Murder Under A Blood Moon

A Mona Moon Mystery
Book Two

Abigail Keam

Worker Bee Press

The history is true. WWI was known as the Great War before 1939.
Mesopotamia refers to the Middle East. The Moon family and
associates, as well as Moon Manor and Bosworth Manor, are
fabrications of my imagination.

Special thanks to Melanie Murphy.

ISBN 978 1 0989383 9 0
5 26 2019

Published in the USA by

Worker Bee Press
P.O. Box 485
Nicholasville, KY 40340

Mona Moon Mysteries

Murder Under A Blue Moon I
Murder Under A Blood Moon II
Murder Under A Bad Moon III

Josiah Reynolds Mysteries

Death By A HoneyBee I
Death By Drowning II
Death By Bridle III
Death By Bourbon IV
Death By Lotto V
Death By Chocolate VI
Death By Haunting VII
Death By Derby VIII
Death By Design IX
Death By Malice X
Death By Drama XI
Death By Stalking XII

Last Chance For Love Romance Series

Last Chance Motel I
Gasping For Air II
The Siren's Call III
Hard Landing IV
The Mermaid's Carol V

1

Madeline Mona Moon sat on the verandah overlooking her four thousand acre horse farm in Lexington, Kentucky, eating buttermilk biscuits slathered in gravy and eggs sunny side up with bacon on the side. It was going to be a busy day. She had an appointment with her lawyer, Dexter Deatherage, to sign legal papers regarding the Moon Enterprises copper mines. Then she was going to tour the farm with her new estate manager. Some of the white plank fences had become a tad shabby, but Mona wasn't looking forward to the inspection. Repairing and repainting the fences would be time consuming and expensive, but it had to be done.

Her personal secretary, Jetta Dressler, poured coffee for them both before going through the morning mail.

"Anything interesting?" Mona asked, reaching under the table to pet Chloe, her standard poodle.

Chloe smelled the bacon and nudged Mona with her wet nose.

Mona broke a crisp piece in two and fed Chloe half. "That's all you get, little missy. Samuel has already fed you your morning breakfast." Mona looked up to find Jetta giving her an impatient stare. "Sorry. You were saying."

Jetta handed over the morning mail. "Just some social invitations and a request to speak at the Lexington Women's Club in July."

"On what subject?"

"They want to hear about your adventures in Mesopotamia."

"I can't think of anything more boring."

Jetta looked amused. "Surely, you can think of something to say—a single woman, carrying a handgun for protection, working in a foreign country surrounded by dangerous men. That in itself would be interesting to most women weighed down by the drudgery of their everyday routine. They're dying to hear from a woman who has actually experienced life."

"They want to know if I was swept up by a dashing sheik on a white charger and spirited into the desert for a romantic interlude like in some picture they saw with Rudolf Valentino."

"Well?"

"And if I rode a camel."

"Let's get back to the handsome sheik."

"I rode a donkey."

"Let's get back to the handsome sheik."

"All I saw were poor, desperate people oppressed by the Ottomans and then the British. They had nothing on their minds but survival."

"Why do you always have to be so practical, so blunt? I wish I could be swept away by some sheik to his private tent for a little canoodling."

"You'd have to share him with his other three wives."

"What?"

"Muslim men are allowed four wives."

"I don't think I'd like that."

Mona grinned. "Be careful what you wish for, Jetta, if it concerns handsome dark-haired men with lascivious designs."

"Like the attractive Lord Farley?"

"What brought his name up?"

"Lord Farley is always bringing you flowers and candy. Those are pretty strong indications he wants to formally court you."

"Phsaw. You make it sound like Farley wants to go steady and pin my sweater. He just wants a new notch on his belt. Well, I'll not give him the satisfaction. He'll tire of chasing me sooner or later and try his luck with some other filly."

"If you say so, but he looks mighty determined."

"Let's talk about something else, shall we? How are the repairs to Moon Manor coming along?" Mona asked referring to the remodeling of her ancestral home after a fire devastated the west wing of the mansion. The cause of the fire had been declared arson, and Mona's previous housekeeper, Mrs. Haggin, had been arrested for the fire. She had also been indicted as a conspirator in the murder of Manfred Michael Moon, Mona's uncle.

Mrs. Haggin's husband, Mr. Archer, fled before he could be thrown into the hoosegow. Mona hoped she had seen the last of his backside forever.

Jetta looked at her notes. "The servants' elevator for the west wing is going to be put in this week. Once installed, they will build the encasement around it."

"Do they have the correct stone?"

"The material will arrive tomorrow, and it is a match for Moon Manor's existing masonry. In fact, it came from the same quarry in Indiana."

"Same color?"

"Exactly the same," Jetta repeated. She was well aware Mona worried about making a mistake restoring Moon Manor to its former glory. Jetta thought she was right to be concerned. Many of the locals considered Mona to be an outsider, and worse, a Yankee. Some Bluegrass stalwarts would be happy to see Mona fall on her face. The sight of a rich and powerful newcomer making a fool of herself would reinforce their dislike of outsiders. It didn't matter that Mona employed over a hundred people and kept them from poverty's door during the Depression, or that she began a health program to rid her workers' children of lice, rickets, and worms—common childhood ailments during the 1930s. All they saw was that Mona was chauffeured about in a red and black Daimler during the week, but didn't go to church on Sunday, even with a driver to take her. Shame. Shame.

While tongues wagged behind Mona's back, everyone was polite after hearing the rumor she kept a gun in her purse and would shoot anyone who looked at her cross-eyed. How folks knew Mona kept a pistol in her purse, Jetta didn't know, but she suspected Mona's Aunt Melanie might have played a part in spreading the gossip.

Jetta eyed Mona eating her breakfast. The sun filtered through the trees highlighting Mona's platinum hair and fair skin, giving her an ethereal quality. Even Mona's golden eyes lent her otherworldliness hard to describe unless one saw it for herself. She knew Mona must realize what people were whispering, but she didn't seem to care, as Mona's facial expression was always one of composure and confidence.

For a moment, Jetta wished she could be more like Mona, but she let her behavior be dictated by others' opinions too often. She was determined to emulate Mona and steer her own future, but Jetta's thoughts were disturbed by Violet, Mona's personal maid, carrying a small silver tray, hurrying out on the verandah.

"Miss Mona, a telegram has come for you," Violet said, breathlessly and obviously dying of curiosity.

Mona picked it up and noticed Violet had stationed herself where she could read it when opened. "Thank you, Violet. That will be all."

"You might need to answer it, Miss Mona. The messenger boy is waitin'."

Mona pried open the envelope. "All right, Violet. Can I read it by myself first?"

Violet stepped back, waiting impatiently. Telegrams were exciting, and Violet wished she would get one someday. She had only received two letters in her entire life and secretly wished for a pen pal from the other side of the world.

"Oh, no!"

"What is it, Miss Mona?" Jetta said, alarmed at Mona's distraught expression. She had never seen Mona so upset.

Mona handed her the beige slip of paper. "It's from my friend, Lady Alice Morrell. She says her life is in danger, and I should come at once."

"Does she say why?" Jetta asked, skimming over the telegram.

"I must go to her. She would never send such

a message if she wasn't in real need." Mona turned to Violet, who quivered with anticipation. "Violet, have Thomas bring my steamer trunks to my room and pack them quickly. I'll keep my appointment with Mr. Deatherage, but when I get back, we'll have Jamison drive us immediately to Cincinnati to catch the express train to New York."

"Us, Miss?"

"I certainly can't go to England without my maid. Whatever you don't have, we'll either purchase on the ship or in London."

"I'm going across the ocean . . . with you?"

Mona turned to Jetta. "I'll need you to make travel arrangements."

"It's very short notice, but I'll do what I can," Jetta replied, a little flustered. She had never made transcontinental preparations before.

"You must do more than that. You must take over the mansion repairs and the running of the farm. Do you think you're up for it?"

"I can try."

"You must do more than try. You must succeed. Of course, you may wire me if you need assistance. Mr. Deatherage will handle all my routine business concerns, but he will help you carry through."

"If you insist."

"I must. There's much to do before I travel this afternoon, so I'll leave you now." Mona stood and gathered the urgent notice from Jetta. "Violet, close your mouth and move."

"Yes, Miss. Right away, Miss." Violet scampered off to find Thomas, the butler.

Jetta said, "Miss Mona, the Western Union boy is waiting for an answer."

Mona's cheeks grew a healthy pink color. "Yes, I must respond to Lady Alice. Thank you for reminding me." She hurried to the front hall and found the messenger waiting patiently.

"Any message, Miss?" he asked, doffing his hat.

"Just say this. Amiens."

"Amen, Miss?"

"No. A M I E N S."

"Is it a who or a what, if you don't mind my asking?"

"Amiens is where the Allied forces launched a counterattack against the Germans in the summer of 1918. It was the beginning of the end for the Great War."

The telegram boy stood dumbfounded. He had written many an odd note in his time, but this was very peculiar. "Yes, but what does it mean?"

"I'm coming!"

2

Mona and Violet were taking in the air on the deck of the USS Iroquois when the ship hit a swell, and they both lost their balance with Violet ending up in the lap of an elderly man sitting in a deck chair. Mona landed in the arms of another man.

"Steady on. Looks like you haven't found your sea legs yet."

Mona looked up in surprise to see a dark, handsome man wearing a gray wool suit—Lawrence Robert Emerton Dagobert Farley. "What are you doing here?"

"I'm going to see an old friend. Fancy meeting you on the same ship, but I must say I do like this," Farley said holding Mona tighter in his arms. "Quite cozy."

"Let go and wipe that smirk off your face."

"Not before you give me a kiss as payment for saving you from a nasty fall."

Mona pulled away, declaring, "You are something of a wolf, Lord Bobby."

"Ah, don't call me that, but if you want to address me on a first name basis, you may call me Robert."

"Farley will do," Mona replied, straightening her hat.

Grinning, Farley stepped over and extricated Violet from the flustered gentleman's lap. He pointed at Violet, now standing beside Mona. "Sorry, old chap. She's American, you know."

"Righto," the man said, as if Violet being American explained it. "If I were twenty years younger, I would have enjoyed it, but the young miss fell on my leg suffering from the gout."

"I'm so sorry," Violet said, embarrassed. "I hope I didn't hurt you."

"Come along, Violet. Let's leave these gentlemen to their conversation." Mona turned and hurried down the deck. The ship hit another swell and the ship listed to the right, causing Mona and Violet to narrowly avoid another mishap.

"Not so fast, ladies," Farley said, catching up with them. He nudged himself between the two women, wrapping his arms around theirs. "You might need a little help in this weather."

"The sea was quite calm when we boarded," Mona said, secretly happy for his assistance. Her stomach was getting a little queasy.

Farley glanced at the darkening sky. "Looks like a storm is coming, so it's going to be a rocky afternoon unless the ship outruns it. Here's a bar. Let's swing in here until the weather settles."

Mona didn't protest as he led them to a table and motioned to a waiter.

"I'll have a Pink Champagne cocktail," Mona ordered.

"Cancel that," Farley said. "A pot of hot tea with three pieces of that vanilla cake I see on the bar."

"Really!" Mona snorted.

"You both look a little green around the gills. Some hot tea and cake will help settle your stomachs."

"So says you," Mona retorted.

Violet said, "Thank you, Lord Farley. I am feeling a little bit off. I think cake might help."

Mona shot Violet a look of disbelief. Her maid was consorting with the enemy.

Satisfied Mona was not going to put up a fight, Farley asked, "What takes such lovely swans on a transatlantic voyage?"

Before Mona could answer, Violet blurted out, "Miss Mona got a telegram from a friend saying her life was in danger."

Mona leaned back in her chair and crossed her arms. She was going to have to speak with Violet about spilling confidential information.

"Whose life is in danger, Violet?"

"A friend in England but I forgot her name."

Violet and Farley turned their attention to Mona.

"Well, give it up, old girl," Farley said.

"I do wish you'd quit referring to me as an old girl or a cow."

"I call you a cow?"

"Frequently."

"If I comply, will you quit referring to me as a nuisance or an annoyance?"

"If I must, but only if you quit being one."

"And no more Lord Bob or Bobby. I hate that."

Mona laughed. "All the more reason."

Farley and Mona's bickering was interrupted by the waiter placing a large pot of hot tea on the table with cups and saucers while another waiter rested plates of vanilla cake with white icing before them.

"This looks so yummy," Violet said, almost licking her lips.

"Dive in, Violet." Farley turned to Mona. "You haven't told me why you are rushing over the pond."

Mona cautioned, "This is strictly sub rosa, mind you."

"Of course. It goes without saying," Farley said, pouring tea into his cup and then milk before pouring for the ladies. He didn't bother pouring milk for them as Americans never took milk with their tea, but they generally took sugar.

"I got word from an old friend. Her father was stationed in Mesopotamia during 1928-29 when I was there my first time."

"You were a brave lass to go there twice."

"One had to go where the work was, but as I was saying before being interrupted."

Farley looked incredulous. "Was that me?"

"His daughter and I worked on an archeological site together and formed a deep bond. She sent me a telegram stating her life is in danger, and I should come post haste."

"Was it like this one?" Farley asked, pulling a crumpled piece of paper out of his pocket and handing it to Mona.

Mona quickly read it. Stunned, she asked, "Alice wrote she knew you, but nothing to indicate you two were close."

"Our family estates lie close together. I grew up with her brother."

"The brother who died in the Battle of the Somme in 1916?"

Farley's face grew dark. "Yes. Precisely. He was the last of the Morrell male line. I joined his brigade when I came of age."

"I didn't know you fought in the Great War."

"It's something I'd rather not discuss."

Taken aback by Farley's heated response to her mentioning the war, Mona took a bite of her cake. It was delicious, and she was glad Farley had ordered it. After several minutes of silence, Mona remarked, "Lady Alice must consider you a great friend to ask you to come and help."

"And you it seems as well."

"Do you know what could be the matter?"

Farley shook his head. "I haven't spoken or written to Alice in six years."

"Why so long?"

"I moved to Kentucky, and we lost touch."

"I see."

"What did Alice write about me?"

Mona answered, "She wrote she did indeed know you and that you were a fine upstanding man."

Farley looked quite pensive. "She would, the darling."

"Is there something I should know, Farley?"

Farley dabbed his face with a napkin and neatly folded it. "Nothing to interest you. Enjoy your cake, but I must be off. Chin-chin, ladies." He walked over to the waiter, telling him to put the bill on his account.

Mona watched him leave the bar. "Well, that was odd, don't you think, Violet?"

"He loves her."

"Who?"

Violet gave Mona a disbelieving look. "Lady Alice."

"I shouldn't think so. He hasn't had any contact with her in years."

Violet smiled tenderly at Mona who wasn't sensitive to the ways of romance. She continued eating her cake, wondering how Mona didn't understand that Lord Farley had possibly loved Lady Alice in the past and his going back to England was painful and conflicted.

It was also obvious to Violet that Lord Farley was now greatly attracted to Mona. She would be interested to watch Lord Farley dance around the two women.

Very interested, indeed.

3

Mona and Violet hurried down the gangplank to customs where Farley waited for them. They shared a cab to the train station and took three overnight compartments to London. Mona had shared a suite with Violet during the sea voyage and now yearned for some privacy with her own room on the train. She was sure Violet felt the same.

After settling in, Mona decided to take dinner in her compartment and was eating from a tray when a knock sounded on her door. Thinking it was the porter to turn down the berth, she said, "Come in."

Farley opened the door. "Hello. I was going to ask you to the dining car, but I see you are already eating."

"I thought I'd pop off to bed early."

He picked up half of a pimento cheese sandwich, taking a bite before making a face and putting the sandwich back on the tray. "This is not enough sustenance, and I'm in need of a steak. Throw a dress on and let's go."

"Does the word please ever enter your vocabulary?"

"Will you *please* put on something that won't embarrass my countrymen and come sup with me?"

"Oh, if you put it nicely that way, how can I refuse?" Mona retorted, curling her lip.

"I'll wait for you in the dining car."

"If you insist."

"I must."

"Go then, so I can change."

"On second thought, I'll wait for you outside your door. I don't trust you to come to the dining car if left alone."

Mona sighed. "Give me a minute."

"A minute only or I'm coming in again."

Mona pushed Farley out the door. Why did he vex her so? He was handsome to be sure and charming, but she had met many a handsome and charming man before, and they had never aggravated her like he did. Mona shook her head. It was a mystery.

It only took her several minutes to put on a black dress with pearls and fix her hair and makeup.

As she stepped from her compartment, Farley looked her up and down, saying, "Ah, my lovely cow."

"I told you not to call me that, and I'm not your lovely anything."

"I hoped you would have had ample time to appreciate my glowing attributes enough that we could let our guard down with each other."

"I haven't witnessed anything but your constant condescension toward Americans."

"Nonsense, my dear. I love Americans. That was my condescension for you."

Mona pulled away from him. "Tell me why I should be going to dinner with you."

"Bloody hell, Mona. Can't you take a joke?"

"I don't like to be teased. I was teased enough as a child. I told you that."

"I'm not your whipping boy. We aren't married, you know."

Mona gave a strong look of disapproval.

"Would you like to spank naughty me?" He raised an eyebrow in anticipation.

"Could you possibly be more uncouth? Let's get on with dinner."

"What did I say now?" Farley said, following Mona to the dining car.

Dinner was civil. Farley relished a medium rare steak with horseradish and all the trimmings while Mona picked at a baked halibut with a light hollandaise sauce drizzled on it. Conversation was mostly about their respective horse farms and their horses. It was polite, genteel, and very mind-numbing. Mona struggled to keep from yawning until she noticed a swarthy man sitting on the other side of the dining car watching them intently.

"All right," Mona said.

"All right what?"

"Go back to being your obnoxious self. You bore me silly being sweet. Dull as dishwater."

"How's this? I was going to catch you off

guard and pinch your bottom on the way out."

"A gentleman never pinches a lady."

"I'm a lord, not a gentleman. If you knew anything about English aristocracy, you'd know we eat and drink ourselves silly until we become crippled with the gout, and we ravish our house-maids indiscriminately, but we never abandon our manners."

"I've run into some of the British upper-class on my travels. Not all of them acted so posh when they tried to peel my knickers off. Down-right feral if you ask me, but then again, men are the same everywhere."

"I pledge to always ask permission before I take your knickers off," Farley said, crossing his heart with his fingers. "Anyone successful?"

"Why do you think I got a gun?"

"So the rumor is true."

Mona patted her clutch. "My little friend goes where I go."

"How did you ever get it through customs?"

"I put it where they'd never expect it of a la-dy."

Farley leaned forward with his chin resting on his hand. "Do tell, saucy wench."

"I think my little pal comes in handy, especially when I am being watched as I am now—or maybe we are being watched."

"Who?"

"Don't turn around, goose. The dark-haired gentleman sitting at the table near the bar at the other end of the car. He's been watching us. I'm sure of it."

"May I have a light?" Lord Farley said to a waiter, giving the dark-haired man a cursory glance when the waiter lit his cigarette.

Mona hissed, "See."

"The dark-haired man with the Van Dyke beard?"

"Yes."

"He seems innocent enough to me. It looks like the man is engrossed in his menu, darling Mona, or perhaps he suffers from gas. You know how the jolting of a train can play with one's gastric system. I like the beard though. Very continental. Do you think I'd look good with a Van Dyke beard?"

"I'm telling you he was burning a hole through me."

"I would ogle you, too, with that hair of yours."

"People do gape at me all the time. I'm used to it. I know my hair is unusual."

"Not to mention your skin is almost white as well. However do you protect yourself from the sun? Get sunburned much?"

Mona leaned forward and whispered. "But the looks I get are from the curious. That man looked at me differently."

"Are you sure it was directed toward you? It could be me, you know."

The waiter brought them a bread basket with little hard butter balls.

Mona tried to spread one on a roll unsuccessfully.

"Look what you've done. You've battered your bun."

Mona put her purse on the table.

Farley grabbed her hand. "I'm taking your concern seriously, but there's no reason this chap has to know. He might have something to do with Alice's situation. Keep an eye on him and if he tries anything funny, I'll take care of him. Put your purse away. There's no room on the table for it, and that little gun you keep in it might accidentally go off and spoil my dinner, not to mention poke a hole in me. Get your mind off him. Let's talk about something pleasant for a change."

Mona realized Farley was as tense as she was. It seemed like it was taking forever to get to London. "We've been crossing swords for days now. You received an alarming message as I did from Alice, yet, you haven't seemed interested in discussing it. Apparently Alice feels she needs both of us to come to her aid, but why? Who would threaten such a lovely woman? This doesn't feel right."

"I know. I wish she had given us more information, but I don't believe Alice could have done anything to cause someone to hate her. It must have something to do with her father."

"Colonel Morrell?" Mona asked.

"Don't act coy with me. If you worked on the same archaeological dig with Alice, you must know what I'm talking about."

Mona lowered her eyes. "Alice had nothing to do with it."

"But you do know about the Colonel?"

"I suspected, but I didn't want to pursue it any further, so I left it alone."

Farley said, "Colonel Morrell was in charge of the dig. You know as well as I do, the old man was smuggling priceless antiquities out of Iraq for the British Museum or the black market."

Mona lowered her voice, glancing at the man near the bar. "That's a very serious charge."

"The British were still in control then, and it would have been very easy for Morrell to hand items off to them."

"I still don't see what this has to do with Alice. Her father has been dead for years now."

"What happened on that dig?"

"Alice and I were thrown together, since we were the only two English speaking women for hundreds of miles, but it was dangerous with the uprisings. The local people didn't comprehend the importance of our work. We couldn't make them understand we were trying to save precious artifacts from fanatics who were smashing everything they considered idolatrous. They were destroying thousands of years of their own people's history, but we were seen as breaking traditional law. Her father stayed behind, but I made Alice come with me to Basra and then we traveled through the Suez Canal to Beirut. From there we got a ship to England. It was only when we arrived at Alice's family home, did we discover her father had been killed in an attack. She was devastated, thinking she had deserted him by returning to England."

"She had no business being there. He never should have taken her."

"Alice was doing important work."

"Digging up dusty old clay tablets to put in old Gertrude Bell's museum?"

"Alice wanted to contribute something to the world. She was tired of being a beautiful ornament waiting to be married off to some dull aristocrat with mush for brains."

"And you say I'm condescending."

"Why are you getting so upset?"

"I guess now I'm going to hear a rousing chorus about women's rights. Baloney, as you Yanks say. Where is Alice now, Mona? Heading toward thirty, unmarried, no child to call her own, and now she is being threatened. She obviously has no close friends in England because she had to beg the two of us to come from across the bloody Atlantic Ocean to help her. That's where Alice is. Alone and afraid." Farley threw down his napkin and fled the dining car, turning his chair over in the rush.

Why had Farley suddenly become so emotional?

Mona stared after him totally baffled. She finished her meal while keeping an eye on the gentleman near the bar. After paying the bill, she headed toward her cabin, pondering on what Farley had said. It seemed there was more going on with His Lordship returning to Great Britain than helping an old friend. She decided to check on him.

Knocking on his door, she opened it without waiting for an answer, afraid he might tell her to go away.

He was staring out the window sipping on a whisky. His hair was tousled and his shirt was open to the waist exposing his muscular chest. His eyes looked smoky and dangerous.

Mona's throat caught.

"What do you want?"

"I'm sorry, Farley. Obviously, I said something to upset you. I forget our jousting can become too fierce sometimes."

"It is I who should apologize, Mona. I've acted foolishly. I'm not mad at you. I'm angry with myself."

"Over Alice?"

"It's too long and boring to go into, my American cow. Maybe some day."

"I see we're back on friendly terms again if you are calling me a cow."

Farley held up a bottle of Glenfiddich. "Nightcap?"

"Don't mind if I do, Lord Bob."

Farley poured Mona a drink and handed the glass to her. "Touché, my American cow." Farley smiled as he and Mona clicked glasses, wondering if he would ever get a second chance at happiness. He had already thrown one chance away. He watched Mona as she sipped her whisky.

Could Mona ever love him?

Would she ever love him?

That was the question Farley wanted answered.

4

Farley helped Mona and then Violet from the train into a sooty, filthy, smoky Victoria Station. Looking about, he took a deep breath, saying, "It's great to be home."

"I see most of the trains don't have diesel engines yet." Mona grabbed a clean handkerchief from her pocket and handed it to Violet. "Hold this up to your face, Violet. Don't breathe in these noxious fumes." Coughing, Mona held a gloved hand to her face.

"I'll see about our trunks," Farley offered, holding out his hand for the ticket stubs.

Violet gratefully gave him the luggage vouchers.

"Come Violet. We'll wait for His Lordship in the waiting area. This is a far cry from Union

Terminal in Cincinnati, I can tell you."

Violet greedily read her travel brochure as they walked down the platform. "Victoria Station opened in 1860. Think of that."

"Let's hurry. I'm choking to death." Mona and Violet swung through some doors leading to a bustling concourse. Violet rushed up to a vendor and handed over money. "One Coca-Cola please."

"Wouldn't you rather have a pot of tea and some nice scones with a bit of strawberry jam and clotted cream?" asked the vendor, wearing a bright blue apron that sported images of Buckingham Palace.

Violet leaned over the counter, searching for any kind of soda pop. "Don't you sell Coca-Cola?"

"We keep some for Americans."

"Please, I need one. My employer is gagging."

"Hmmm," the vendor replied, peering over her glasses and flipping off the top of a bottle. "Here you go, ducky. Enjoy your stay with us."

Hurrying back, Violet handed the soda to Mona. "I'm sorry, Miss, but it's warm."

Mona took a long swallow of the soda, waited

a few seconds and then took another swig. "That's the way they serve drinks over here. They don't use much ice. It is considered an American custom."

"Who wants to drink a warm Coca-Cola?"

"You get used to it." Mona took another sip. "Ah, that's better. I don't know why but a frog got caught in my throat. Silly of me."

"The air was awfully foul, Miss Mona."

"Quite."

"I see some open seats. Let's wait for Lord Farley over there."

"A good idea, but I was expecting Lady Alice to meet us. We telegrammed from Plymouth when we would be arriving. I hope she didn't get the train stations mixed up."

"MONA! MONA!"

Mona and Violet turned to see a woman with raven tresses, dressed in a navy suit and hat with ostrich feathers rush over to them.

"Alice!" Mona cried.

Lady Alice clasped Mona in a tight embrace. "Oh, my darling. It's so good to see you. Let me look at you." Alice held Mona at arm's length. "You look fine. Kentucky must agree with you."

"Being rich agrees with me," Mona chuckled.

"When you wrote about your good fortune, I was so happy for you. Are you still pleased, Mona?"

"I'm settling in, but let me look at you." Mona noticed the cuffs on Alice's sleeves were a little frayed and a button was missing from her jacket. "Still beautiful as ever with your black hair and light blue eyes."

Alice twittered, "We look like salt and pepper shakers, don't we? I with my ebony hair and you with your ivory hair. We make quite the pair. We must have a long chat. So much has happened since I last saw you."

Mona nodded. "Lady Alice. This is my maid, Violet."

Violet did her best to curtsy and said, "How do you do, Lady Alice?"

"Curious," Lady Alice said, looking oddly at Violet.

Mona leaned over and whispered, "You don't have to curtsy, Violet. You're an American and hardly anyone practices it anymore except to royalty."

Violet said, "Miss Mona gave me a book by

Jane Austen to read."

Lady Alice laughed. "Well, Jane Austen was before my time. Don't look so crestfallen, young lady. I once tripped before His Majesty at a ball when meeting his son, David."

"You mean the Prince of Wales?" Violet asked, dumbstruck.

"Exactly."

"I've seen pictures of him in the Saturday Evening Post. He is so handsome."

Lady Alice raised an eyebrow and replied, "Among other things, I hear."

"Do tell," Mona said.

Alice looked about. "I'll have to tell you about a Mrs. Simpson and the Prince of Wales. She's an American, you know."

"I didn't know, but I can't wait to hear. There's been nothing about them in the American press."

"It's supposed to be very hush hush, but it's common knowledge." Alice scanned the crowd. "Is this everyone?"

"Farley is getting our trunks," Mona explained. "Here he comes now."

Alice swung around to see Farley come

through the doors with porters following him.

Farley froze when he saw Alice.

"Robert," Alice gasped as she rushed to embrace him, holding him close until she sobbed.

"Alice?" Farley said.

Alice reached for a handkerchief and dabbed her eyes. "I'm such a silly goose, but I'm so happy my dearest friends are here. The last six months have been such a strain."

Mona said, "About your telegram, Alice."

Alice's face clouded. "Not here. Not now. You can never tell who's listening." She entwined her arms around Mona and Farley. "My driver is outside. Let us be off. With luck we should be home by tea time."

Farley beckoned to the porters to follow while Violet trailed behind the threesome. She noticed the heels on Lady Alice's shoes were worn down and the back of her skirt hung unevenly. Lady Alice either had a terrible maid or she had no maid at all. A lady in her position always had someone tending to her clothes . . . unless something was wrong.

The sight of seeing Lady Alice dressed so shabbily embarrassed Violet, but that was not the only thing which distressed her. She couldn't help but notice a swarthy man with a Van Dyke beard watching them intently. He wore a three piece, brown suit tailored to perfection and made from the finest wool. He wore a gold bracelet on his right hand and his cuff links looked gold as well. The man was obviously not English, but Violet couldn't place his nationality. She tried to get Mona's attention, but when the stranger saw Violet noticing him, he folded his newspaper and calmly walked in the other direction.

Violet stopped and searched the crowd, biting her bottom lip in consternation. Perhaps she was confused. The man was probably looking at something in her direction which had nothing to do with her. After all, she was in a strange country when she had never been farther than twenty miles from her home before. It was only natural she was tense.

"Violet, come on. The car is waiting," Mona said, poking her head inside the station's door, looking for her maid.

"Coming, Miss," Violet said, wondering if she should mention the man. It didn't matter because she forgot about him when she jumped into the front seat of Lady Alice's Rolls-Royce, busy looking at the sites of London.

If only her mother could see her now.

5

Lady Alice acted gay in the car, keeping the conversation light. Mona and Farley responded in kind while Violet chit-chatted with the chauffeur until he complained he needed to concentrate and that she prattled on like a magpie. So much for merry old England.

Before long, they progressed from the crowded streets of London to the lush, green countryside. The trip took longer than expected as the Rolls had to slow down for sheep in the road, veer around bicyclists on holiday, and make several stops for the ladies at various pubs along the way to use the facilities. Finally, the car turned on the road leading to Bosworth Manor, named after the Battle of Bosworth, which was where Lady Alice's ancestor fought alongside Henry

Tudor who defeated Richard III for the throne of England in 1485.

Mona noticed that many fields lay fallow and several tenant houses looked vacant. The estate had certainly run down since she had last been here. Mona glanced at Farley who had a concerned expression on his face as he gazed out the window, but neither of them commented.

Grabbing Alice's hand, Mona gave her an encouraging smile.

Alice explained, "The place doesn't look the way it used to, does it, Mona? Death taxes after father died. They cleaned me out, I'm afraid."

Farley said, "You should have let me know, Alice."

"How could I confide in you, Robert? You were on the other side of the world."

Mona noticed the intensity of their words. It wasn't so much what they said, but how Alice and Farley addressed each other. There was an intimacy in their tone that imparted a long and close relationship. Mona looked away embarrassed, not from their encounter, but because she felt a tinge of jealousy. The swell of emotion startled her.

"We'll talk about it later," Farley said heatedly as the car drove up to Alice's ancestral home.

Bosworth Manor was as Mona remembered it—a red brick monstrosity built in the 1500s, which was drafty, cold, and uncomfortable. It barely boasted of modern plumbing, and electricity had been installed by Alice's father under protest, only because overnight guests complained. If Bosworth Manor hadn't been deemed a historical building, Mona would have encouraged Alice to tear it down and build a smaller, more modern home.

The car pulled up the drive and stopped at the front door. The chauffeur jumped out to open the back door. Violet was apparently left to her own devices.

Stiff from the journey, Mona stretched to work out the kinks in her back. She was tired and wanted only to go to her room.

The main entrance to Bosworth Manor opened and the butler stepped out. "Lady Alice. I see your trip to London was successful. All is in readiness for your guests."

"Thank you, George."

"Of course. Welcome back, Your Lordship. A

pleasure to see you as always, Miss Mona."

"Nice to see you again, George."

"I trust your trip was pleasant, Miss Mona."

"It was tiring."

"I see. I will have everyone's bags taken to their rooms." George looked expectantly at Violet.

"Oh, George, this is my maid, Violet. Take care of her, will you?"

"My pleasure, Miss Mona."

Alice said, "We could do with a bit of something."

"Tea has been set up in the study, Lady Alice."

"Good. Has the fire been lit?"

"Yes, Lady Alice."

Alice nodded. "Let's get something to eat and then have a lie-down."

"Sounds perfectly wonderful," Mona agreed. "Alice, I hope we're not having a formal dinner tonight. I just don't have it in me."

"Quite right. Dinner will be at nine and casual. A day frock will do. George, tell cook to keep it simple tonight."

"Very good, Lady Alice."

"Thank you," Mona said over her shoulder to Alice, following George into the house.

Farley escorted Alice into the manor where they found Mona was already helping herself to a cup of tea and a large slice of lemon cake with several finger sandwiches in the study.

"Move over, Mona. I'm starved as well," Alice said, sliding beside Mona on a settee. "Robert, shall I pour for you?"

"I'd rather have a whisky, if you don't mind. I'll get it myself."

"Very well. Suit yourself. You always do."

Again, Mona noticed the tension between them and decided to change the subject.

"What about Violet? I see George already has her working," Mona said, spying Violet toting luggage through the opened door.

"George will take care of her," Alice assured.

"Violet's very young and has never been outside Kentucky before," Mona said, wondering why the luggage hadn't been driven around to the servants' entrance and taken up the back stairs to their rooms.

Alice shut the door to the study. "That brings to mind other issues. I see you didn't bring your valet, Robert. Can you dress yourself? I have no man to assist you."

"Not a problem."

"Mona, I noticed you were observing the servants taking the luggage up the main staircase. It's easier on them than going to the back of the manor and lugging the trunks up the narrow back staircase."

"Alice, there were fields not mowed and several vacant houses on the estate. What's going on?" Mona asked.

"Life, Mona. Life. I've been hit with difficulties no ordinary woman should face."

"But I was here four years ago, and Bosworth Manor seemed in fine fettle."

"I was struggling financially long before then. I could just hide it better, but the bottom fell out with the crash of 1929."

"Tell us what happened," Farley said.

"If only my brother had lived, Robert. He would have managed the estate so much better than I." Alice wiped away a tear. "I have muddled so badly."

Farley poured some of his whisky into her teacup. "Here, you need this more than I."

Alice gratefully took a sip.

"Don't keep us in the dark, Alice," Mona encouraged.

"Things began to slide after my brother died. Father was sick with grief, causing him to make bad investments. To make matters worse, it was difficult to find tenants. So many young men died in the Great War and then the Spanish Flu right after, so it was hard to replace the older farmers who either died or retired. After Father passed on, the death duties took what little reserve the estate still possessed. The truth is I'm not only broke, but deeply in debt. That's all there is to it. I've had to let go many of the servants including my maid. There is only a skeleton staff left."

Mona thought back to Colonel Morrell smuggling Sumerian and Babylonian artifacts out of Mesopotamia and now understood why. He was trying to save Bosworth Manor. "Whatever shall you do, Alice?"

"I intend to sell, but who would want this broken down place? After four hundred years of the family line, I will be the Morrell to lose Bosworth Manor."

Mona offered, "I can lend you money."

"Oh, darling, that is very kind, but nothing you could loan me would be enough. This place is a money pit. Thank you, but no." Alice looked wistfully about the room. "I'm afraid Bosworth Manor is out of step with the modern world."

Mona looked at Farley. "You haven't said anything. What do you think?"

Farley asked, "If you don't want a loan, why have you summoned us, Alice?"

"I feel my life is in danger, Robert. That's the reason."

"How so?" Mona asked, suddenly fearful. Alice was very dear to her and the closest thing to a sister that Mona would ever have.

Alice rose and closed all the drapes before locking the study door. Taking a key from a chain around her neck, Alice went over to a wall and pressed on a hidden lever. A panel slid back revealing a door that Alice unlocked. "This is an old priest hole the family converted into a safe. We keep all of our important papers in here."

Mona and Farley followed Alice into the room where three walls of shelves held the Morrell ancestral archives. In the middle of the room sat a carved wooden desk with one chair and one electric light.

Dazzled by the documents lining the walls, Mona picked up an official looking scroll and studied the seals hanging from it. "This is from the time of Henry VIII." She picked up another one with a broken seal and unrolled it, reading the faded cursive script. "Oh, my word. This is an appeal to Elizabeth I not to reinstate the Oath of Supremacy of 1559. This document alone is priceless."

Farley said, "Sorry, old girl, but every great estate has documents like this hoarded in some drafty attic or whatnot. These letters are trifles, Mona. Let's stay on track."

Mona felt heat rise from her chest to her cheeks. "Of course. Alice, what did you want to show us?"

Alice said, "Your reaction reminds me of our time in Iraq. You were always so excited when we found something of importance. You have such a love of history. It's nice to see it hasn't faded."

"Alice," Farley barked.

"Be patient, Robert." Alice took another key and unlocked the desk drawer where she pressed on the side panel and a hidden door sprang open, revealing a cubby hole.

Mona clapped her hands together. "Secret rooms within secret rooms. Clever."

"Ingenious, yes," Alice agreed. She pulled four letters from the cubby hole and handed them to Farley. "I've been getting these for some time now."

He quickly perused one and handed it to Mona, who read it quickly.

"Are they all like this?" Mona asked, reading another one Farley handed to her.

"Yes," Alice replied.

"Give us what we want or you will die," Mona read out loud. "Do you know to what they are referring or who 'us' might be?"

Alice shook her head.

"Is this all of them?" Farley asked.

"I threw away the first three thinking they were pranks."

Mona asked, "Were they the same?"

"The sender threatened to place me under a curse. They were frightful to read."

"I can imagine," Mona remarked.

"How were the envelopes postmarked?" Farley asked.

"All of the envelopes were stamped from

London, but the last two were mailed from the closest village to Bosworth Manor. That's when I became frightened. Whoever has been sending those is now here."

Flipping over the envelopes and studying the postmarks, Mona said, "When was the last post date?"

"Just last month."

"You telegrammed us a little over two weeks ago, so you weren't immediately spooked. What happened to make you finally contact us?"

"The manor was broken into and ransacked."

"Terrible," Mona said.

"That's not the worst of it. My Great Dane was killed and one of my house servants was knocked unconscious and beaten. There was a message scrawled in lipstick on the dressing table in my room stating, 'You're next.'"

"How could have that happened with the staff present?" Mona asked.

"My staff and I were attending a local fair. Only my man Jansen was here. He stayed behind because he had an ulcer on his foot."

"Is he all right?"

"Yes, Mona, and thank God for such a blessing. He was back on his feet two days later, but quit soon after, and I don't blame him."

"I'm very sorry about your dog. I know you were very attached to him."

Alice's eyes teared up. "It was a shock but I think he tried to protect Jansen and was killed in the process."

"You say Jansen was knocked unconscious and then beaten. Why would he be beaten if he was already unresponsive?" Farley asked.

"Robert, I don't know. I can only go by his statement to the police. Jansen said he was struck from behind and that's all he remembers until he woke up in the hospital."

"It's not unusual for traumatized victims not to remember a chain of events. What worries me is this miscreant was roaming about your house. Was the manor thoroughly searched?" Mona asked.

Farley put the letters in his pocket. "Your house was being watched and is probably now as well."

"Do you have any idea what *they* may want, Alice?" Mona asked, handing Farley the last letter.

"No idea."

"Was anything taken?"

"Just a few of my jewels, but nothing else, or at least, as far as I can tell. There are still a few important paintings I own—two Reynolds, one Turner, and several by Joseph Wright, but they weren't touched, but the house was turned upside down, even the servants' rooms."

"You sound as though you don't believe robbery was the aim," Mona said.

"I think the break-in was to frighten me, and the prowler didn't know Jansen would be in the house with the dog. The intruder was surprised and it escalated from there."

Mona asked, "Where is Jansen now?"

"He's working at the pub in the village."

Farley grunted, shoving the last letter into his inside pocket for safekeeping.

Alice started to speak, but stopped.

Mona could tell Alice was reluctant to ask Farley for the letters.

"What jewels were taken?" Farley asked.

"A strand of pearls that were my mother's, a costume bracelet, a rather gaudy piece of jewelry I picked up overseas, and my amethyst ring."

Surprised, Farley asked, "You kept the amethyst ring?"

"I told you I would never part with it, Robert."

Farley smiled tenderly at Alice.

Again, Mona felt she was intruding on a private moment between Farley and Alice as an awkward silence hung in the air. It was unnerving to witness their intimacy.

Mona backed out of the priest hole and sat down on a couch in the study, downing her tea and eating another cucumber sandwich. She was bewildered by her confusion and anger. Why did she feel that way?

Several minutes later, Alice escorted Farley from the priest hole, locked the door, and moved the wall panel back into place.

Sitting beside Mona, Alice refreshed her tea and nibbled a small cake.

"You know we are missing a clue here," Mona finally said, unable to stand the strained quiet.

"What's that, dear?"

"The intruder knew which room was yours."

"It would be easy to deduce. No one sleeps on the second floor but me, now that my maid is gone. The staff sleeps on the third floor. All the intruder had to do was merely peek inside each bedroom and find the only occupied one."

"That takes time. I still think it was an inside job," Mona said, puzzled by the entire affair. Her head was throbbing from the stress of the long journey. She felt a major migraine coming on and needed to rest.

"I think Mona might be on to something, Alice," Farley said. "What about new people in the village or surrounding estates? Anything strange happening?"

"We've become a big tourist area, especially for Americans. Some of the estates have opened their gardens to sightseers, so there are strangers hereabouts every day."

Mona asked, "Have you seen a swarthy man with a Van Dyke beard?"

Alice chirped, "Mona, you've been reading too many detective novels—a dark-skinned man with a Van Dyke beard. Such a cliché."

"I saw him, too," Farley concurred. "He was well-dressed with Western clothes and haircut, but he looked like he was from the Near East."

"That describes several people nearby. We

have all sorts of people from every religion and ethnicity now. Refugees came here after the Great War. My little part of the world has become quite cosmopolitan."

"Have you noticed anything else out of the ordinary?" Mona asked.

"Nothing. It's quite vexing. Perhaps I'm over-reacting."

Farley clasped his hands behind him. "I would take these threats seriously, Alice. You were right to ask for help. What did the local police say about the letters?"

Alice seemed embarrassed. "I didn't tell them, Robert."

"Why not?"

"Because if I had, it would have been all over the village in a matter of days. Our police are not equipped to handle delicate matters. They came about the break-in and that was it."

"What did they make of the threat written on your dressing table mirror?"

"I wiped it off before they came. They never saw it."

Farley asked, "Did you notify Scotland Yard about the letters?"

"I thought to handle it myself until the break-in."

Farley made a clicking noise with his teeth before sipping on his drink. Farley's tenseness cast a pall over the room.

Mona asked, "Do you think any of the discharged servants could be nursing a grudge?"

"I don't know. Perhaps. I just don't know," Alice said, obviously overwrought.

Mona put down her teacup and folded her napkin. "That's enough for now. I think we're tired and in need of a long nap before dinner. You said casual, Alice?"

"Dinner is at nine. A day frock will be fine tonight." Alice rang the servants' bell.

A knock on the door sounded and George entered. "Yes, Miss."

"Please show my guests to their rooms."

"Very good. Follow me, please."

"George, where have you stashed my maid?" Mona asked.

"I've put her in a room on the third floor sharing with a parlor maid."

"Would you tell her to come for me at eight?"

"My pleasure, Miss."

"See you two later tonight." Mona rose and followed George up the grand staircase, wondering if Farley would follow.

He didn't.

6

Violet poked her head inside the room. "Time to dress for dinner, Miss," she said, going over to a wardrobe and pulling out a frock.

"Let me splash some water on my face and put on some makeup." Mona went into the bathroom and performed her ablutions while talking through the door. "Have you settled in, Violet?"

"Yes, Miss."

"How are your accommodations?"

"I don't like to complain, but they're awful. I'm in a room with a housemaid who resents sharing with me."

"I find it odd. Lady Alice said she had cut the staff so there should be free bedrooms."

"Perhaps the maid is to keep an eye out because they think I might filch the silver."

"I'll speak with George tomorrow and tell him I need you close by and have you moved to the second floor."

"Thank you. Even though it's summer, I have to have a blanket. The room is quite chilly."

"The English like their houses cold. Most of these old manors still don't have central heating."

"Does it ever stop raining and warm up, Miss?"

"It can get quite hot in the summertime. Bosworth Manor was built with local stone and the red brick was added as a façade later when brick became the fashion. The window placements were designed to catch cross air breezes. Works better than most modern air-conditioning systems."

Mona came out of the bathroom and sat before the dressing table, running fingers through her tangled platinum tresses. "Can you do something with me, Violet? I've got bed hair."

"Why don't you sweep it up tonight? I can brush it out tomorrow."

"Splendid." Mona patted face powder on with a large powder puff before brushing a slight hint of rouge on her cheeks and applying mascara. "Violet, I've got a favor to ask."

"Yes?"

"I couldn't help but observe Lady Alice's outfit seemed the worse for wear."

"I noticed also."

"You're so good at alterations. While we're at dinner each night and when Lady Alice is away from the house, I want you to go into her closet and rummage through her clothes. No doubt many of them need mending. Also pull out shoes that are worn down. I noticed her shoes today needed a little help, too."

"I'll be very discreet, Miss Mona. I take it she doesn't have a lady's maid."

"Not anymore."

"You can count on me. I'll make her outfits look right as rain."

"I'll have Farley take Lady Alice on a walk or something to get her out of the house."

Mona leaned toward the mirror and put on her lipstick—Passion Pink.

Violet slipped a dress over Mona's head and arms before giving her hair a finishing touch. "Just needs one more thing." Violet snipped a daylily from an arrangement and put it in Mona's hair. "Goes perfectly with your dress." Violet stood back and admired her handiwork.

"Here goes nothing. I want to have dinner over and get to bed again. I have a feeling tomorrow will be strenuous."

"Shall I wait up for you, Miss Mona?"

"You look tired, Violet. Go to bed and try to sleep. I'll make sure you are moved next to me tomorrow."

"I'm going to pull some of Lady Alice's things tonight. At least, take a good look at her shoes."

"Make sure you do your mending in my room. Don't take Lady Alice's things back to your room or the downstairs servants' common rooms. The staff might accuse you of stealing."

"I'll put Lady Alice's items in your chest of drawers until I finish mending them."

"Good idea." Mona took a deep breath and glanced in a full length mirror checking the lines on the back of her stockings. "Not too bad for a commoner."

"You look fabulous, Miss Mona."

"I do, don't I?" Mona replied, grinning. "I'll see you in the morning, Violet. Pleasant dreams."

"Good night, Miss Mona."

Mona left the bedroom and headed toward the staircase when a sudden movement caught her attention in the shadows of the darkened hallway. Searching the wall for a light switch, she called out, "Hello. Anyone there?" She flicked on the lights. Nothing. Mona felt uneasy. Next time she ventured anywhere in the house, she would take her purse—the one which carried her little friend and its six rounds of bullets.

If an intruder could sneak up on a full grown man and a Great Dane, Mona wasn't going to take any chances. Someone had murder on his mind, and Mona was going to ferret him out before he caused Lady Alice any harm.

7

Dinner was uneventful. Afterwards, Mona, Alice, and Farley retired to the library where they had a few drinks and played hearts. Still exhausted from their trip, Farley and Mona begged off around midnight, and Farley escorted the ladies upstairs.

Mona took off her frock and laid it neatly on a hanger in the wardrobe. She read a few chapters of her new Dorothy L. Sayers mystery before drifting off, but she tossed and turned, as her dreams were troubled by murky and disturbing images of being chased.

Regardless, Mona awoke feeling refreshed and studied the play of morning sunlight on the patterned wallpaper when Violet opened the door slightly and peeked in before coming into the room. "Everyone is up and about, Miss."

"Are they down to breakfast?"

"They are about to start."

"Tell Lady Alice not to wait on me. I'll be down in a jiffy."

Violet nodded slowly and seemed reluctant to leave.

"Violet, you look positively green around the gills. What's wrong?"

"It's their breakfast, Miss. It's not like we have back home."

Amused, Mona sat up and patted the bed. "Come here and tell me all about it."

"I don't like to complain."

Mona tried not to smile, knowing Violet loved to grumble. "You're not complaining. You're just telling me the facts as you see them."

Violet sat on the bed. "It's a large meal to be sure, but they eat luncheon items in the morning."

"Like what for instance?"

"They have eggs and fried bread, but there's something on the buffet table called black pudding and it looks horrible."

"Blood pudding does look disgusting but is

actually quite nourishing. It is a combination of cereal, pork blood, animal suet, and herbs."

Violet's brow furrowed.

"What else horrifies you?"

"Fried tomatoes and baked beans for breakfast! Then there are those stinky little fish with their heads and tails still on."

"The fish are called kippers. A kipper is a herring which is pickled and cold smoked. The English love them. If Lady Alice was to come to Moon Manor, we would serve grits and hoecakes for breakfast. It would be just as dissimilar for her as you eating kippers and baked beans for breakfast. That's one of the nice things about traveling. You get to try different things, different foods, and have different experiences."

Mona could see Violet was still pouting. "What's this really about, Violet?"

"You know I love fried tomatoes and could stand a bowl of beans topped with a nice poached egg. All I got was a sloppy bowl of mush with a side of dried out rye bread. I asked the cook was this all I was to get, and she told me to like it or else. Last night I had only two boiled potatoes and some cabbage. A body can't live on that. At least, I can't. At home, the staff eats much the same as you, Miss. Why is it so different here?"

"What were the other servants eating?"

"The same as they served me. Two potatoes each with some cabbage for supper and mush this morning. Aw, it's horrible in the servants' quarters. Everyone is so grumpy and tired. It's because they're not getting enough to eat."

At first, Mona thought Violet was being childish, but maybe Alice's finances were so tight, she could barely feed her servants. Mona couldn't enjoy her breakfast if she suspected the servants were eating only mush. No doubt they would eat the leftovers from breakfast, but that put a strain on Alice, Farley, and herself. How could Mona enjoy her kippers . . . and Mona liked kippers . . . if she knew the staff was getting no protein?

This would not do. Mona jumped out of bed and opened her purse, pulling out twenty pounds. "Violet, have one of the lads take you into the village. Use the entire amount as I don't know how long we'll be here, but get anything the kitchen might need . . . flour, sugar, baking powder, meat, vegetables, fruit . . . and chocolates. You must have chocolates. Explain to the staff that Lord Farley and I are giving them a gift because we know we are adding to their burden, and we wish to repay them for their hard work."

Violet tucked the twenty pound note into her brassiere. "Will you ask Lady Alice about switching my room?"

"I will speak to George, rest assured. Now scoot. I must hurry if I'm to make breakfast." Mona rushed into the bathroom to put her face on and comb her hair. Within several minutes, Mona had freshened up, put makeup on, and donned a beige walking skirt with a white cotton blouse, finishing with a beige sweater with horses embroidered around the cuffs. She topped off the outfit with her mother's wedding necklace and a gold charm bracelet sporting a collection of poodles, the Statue of Liberty, and a bourbon barrel as little reminders of home. She had chosen an understated mode of dress for the country, in other words ... English. All she needed to complete the ensemble was a walking staff and some dogs to accompany her on a gentle trek through the estate.

She hurried down the stairs and, bursting into

the dining hall, made way to the food on the buffet. "Good morning. It's a glorious day, isn't it?"

"Yes, it is," Alice said, sitting across from Farley, who was reading the morning *Daily Telegraph*.

"I was beginning to wonder if you were going to sleep all day," Farley said, looking up from the paper.

"And a gracious good morning to you, too."

Alice mused, "Robert was always grouchy in the morning. Remember how my brother practically woke up singing, and you would bark at everyone until your second cup of coffee. Those were glorious times before the war when we were all together."

"Really?" Mona commented, filling her plate from the dishes on the buffet table. "How interesting. Think of it. Farley being an irritant." Mona sat next to Alice and dove into her food.

Farley made a face. "Woman, you're practically bolting your breakfast."

"I'm famished. Speaking of food, I've sent Violet to the village. Now don't be angry with me, Alice darling, but I'm having her purchase a few items for the staff. It's our way of saying thank you, isn't it, Farley?"

Farley appeared flummoxed for a moment but then rebounded. "Umm, yes, it is. I hope you don't mind, Alice."

"But you shouldn't be thanking me. I'm the one in your debt."

Between bites, Mona said, "It's an American custom, so don't fight me on this."

"You never did so when you came to stay with me previously."

Mona laughed. "I never had any money before. Poor as a church mouse, I was always bumming a pound or two off you and even borrowing your clothes." Mona placed her hand on Alice's arm. "Let Farley and me do this, okay?"

"Well, if you insist."

Farley said, "We do. It's settled then. No more talk about it."

Mona asked, "What is the plan today?"

"I'm waiting on a car I ordered to be delivered," Farley announced.

"That is so extravagant!" Alice gasped.

"It's only a rental. Don't get your knickers in a

knot, Alice. After breakfast, I want to go over your books, so I can see where you stand. Then let's go to your bank and see what can be done."

"I've already done so, Robert," Alice replied with a look of exasperation.

"I hate to say this, but how the bank treats you and how they will treat me acting as your intermediary will have two different results."

Alice expressed disgust. "No truer words were ever spoken. It may be 1933, but it's still a man's world. Even though we English women can now vote and keep our property separate from our husbands', we are still second class citizens. Most unjust."

Farley said, "The world is what it is. Let's not start a revolution today."

"But it's a daily struggle for women, Farley. You have no idea," Mona said between bites of her kippers.

"Hey, I'm on your side. I'm all for letting the women drive the car. I'm perfectly happy to sit in the back seat."

"Mona, I'm afraid we are ganging up on poor Robert."

"I enjoy seeing him squirm."

"I'm waving the white flag, ladies," Farley said, folding his paper.

"What's in the paper, Farley?" Mona asked, trying to snatch part of it.

Farley grabbed it out of her reach. "Wiley Post is going to fly around the world again in July, but this time solo. He's trying for a record of seven days. His plane is called the Winnie Mae."

"Where's he taking off?"

"From Floyd Bennett Field in New York."

"What else?"

"Your President Roosevelt is stirring things up with his New Deal proposals."

"Isn't he your president, too, Farley?"

"I'm still a British subject."

Alice interjected, "I read where he announced the creation of four million public works projects. One of the projects is going to be a bridge across the San Francisco Bay. It is going to be the longest suspension bridge in the world."

Mona replied, "They've been trying to build that bridge for decades. California never could fund it. I submitted a prospectus to survey the proposed route six years ago. They rejected it."

"How dare they turn down a then twenty-

three-year-old woman with practically no experience to survey one of the longest bridges in the
world," Farley said.

"Oh, shut up," Mona said. She stuck her
tongue out at him.

He stuck his tongue out at her as well.

"I'll believe that bridge will be built when I see
it," Mona said.

"What else is happening in America?" Alice
asked.

"We have twenty-five percent unemployed.
There was a run on the banks when Roosevelt
took us off the gold standard and made it illegal
to privately own gold. People are literally starving.
The farmland in the Midwest is drying up and
creating huge dust clouds that cover entire towns.
Other than that, we're fine."

"There were runs on the banks before Roosevelt took office," Farley said.

"Because he threatened to take us off the gold
standard in his speeches running for president."

Farley countered, "Roosevelt is going to be a
godsend for American, Mona. Mark my words."

"I hope so. I voted for him."

Alice replied, "Great Britain went off the gold

standard in 1931. Things are bad here as well."

"Enough of this banter. We can't solve the world's problems by sitting on our duffs. Let's get to work," Farley said.

"I think I'll go through your father's correspondence. May I have the keys?" Mona asked.

Handing over the keys, Alice said, "Yes, but keep the study door locked while the priest hole is exposed. I don't want the servants to know about the room."

"Let's be off, Alice. I want to look at your accounts," Farley said, rising from his chair.

"The books are in the steward's office, not far from here. We can walk it easily."

Farley added, "Hopefully, my car will be delivered by the time we're finished. Keep an eye out for it, Mona. Chin chin."

Alice and Farley left, whereupon George entered the dining room to clear the buffet. Surprised to see Mona still eating, he asked, "Do you wish anything else, Miss?"

Mona took a long sip of her orange juice, dabbed her mouth, and folded her napkin. "Tell cook the breakfast was fine."

"Very good, Miss."

"Oh, George. Will you bring my maid's things down to the room next to me?"

"That's most irregular, Miss. I've already assigned her a room."

"Yes, I know, but we're going to buck tradition this trip. By the way, send word to Violet I wish to see her now."

"Danny has taken her to the village. She said she had some errands to run."

"Have Violet's things moved by the time she gets back. Thank you, George."

"Shall I tell her you wish to see her when she returns?"

"On second thought, no. Violet has her instructions. I will be in the study, and I don't want to be disturbed."

"Very good, Miss. Shall I expect you for luncheon?"

"Yes, and probably Lady Alice and Lord Farley will join me as well. What time is lunch?"

"Half past noon, Miss."

"Very good. Oh, George, Lord Farley is expecting a rental car to be delivered. Take care of it, will you?"

"Yes, Miss."

"Thank you."

"Will that be all, Miss?"

Mona rose and reached for the paper. "I'll ring if I need something."

"Yes, Miss."

Mona left the dining hall and crossed the great hall to the study. She closed and locked the study's two massive doors and pulled the drapes shut in case a curious servant decided to peek in the windows. She slid back the panel and unlocked the door to the priest hole. It was very tempting to spend the day studying 400-year-old documents, but Mona knew time was of the essence. Perhaps Alice would let her roam through the family archives once the mystery of the threatening letters had been solved.

Mona sat at the desk and murmured, "Where do I begin?"

She leaned back in the leather swivel chair with her elbows on the armrests surveying the room. Knowing Alice had gone through her father's correspondence and finding nothing that would shed light on the current problem, it seemed to Mona that Colonel Morrell might have hidden something significant in this alcove. What better place to hide a secret than in a clandestine priest hole?

Wondering where Colonel Morrell might hide a precious document, Mona was drawn to the desk. It looked very old. Mona knew desks made in the seventeenth and eighteenth centuries frequently had many secret drawers to hide valuables. She unlocked the concealed cubby hole Alice had shown her and found nothing.

Mona stared at the desk. There must be more hidden spaces. She knocked on the wood listening for a difference in the sound and caressed the wood with her fingertips feeling for a lever or a depression in the wood. Again, nothing.

Frustrated, she scooted her chair away from the desk and studied it. It must have been the desk of a sea captain or someone connected with overseas commerce. It had ships, dolphins, spouting whales, and oranges carved into the sides.

Mona thought it odd for the Morrells to possess such a desk. She knew something of the family's background and knew they had never enlisted in the navy as a career or invested in seafaring trade. They had made their wealth from renting their land and the wool trade from sheep.

Hmmm, maybe Colonel Morrell picked it up on his many adventures. He had traveled extensively, and his father had gone on the grand tour of Europe as young wealthy men did in the nineteenth century. Mona would ask Alice about the desk at lunch.

Still, Mona was not giving up. She got on her hands and knees with a magnifying glass she found on one of the wall shelves and searched for a cabinetmaker's mark or something that would point to the desk's origin. Slowly she made her way around the desk until she came to its right side panel. Mona knocked on the panel. It sounded hollow. Excited, she felt around the edges and then pressed on the various objects carved. Nothing happened.

Flummoxed, Mona sat on the floor. Mona was positive a secret compartment was built into the side, but how to get to it was the question. She pondered for a long time before hitting upon the idea of pressing the carvings in a specific order. She tried various combinations and failed.

"Perhaps the carvings tell a story," she muttered, knowing oranges were considered a rarity in the sixteenth through eighteenth centuries, causing men to risk their lives for them. "If this is a seafaring captain's desk, he sails in his ship, sees whales and dolphins on his way to pick up oranges." Mona pressed on the carvings in that order. She heard something give way, so she pressed harder. A panel sprang open.

"Eureka!" Mona cried. "I've done it." She carefully pried open the panel door and looked. A dusty, red leather book lay inside. Mona gingerly pulled it out and opened it. It was Colonel Morrell's private journal. She turned to one of the last pages and read Colonel Morrell's scrawling cursive handwriting.

I finally got word that Alice and Mona arrived in England. Knowing my dearest daughter is safe, I told MS no more. He was not happy and threatened me. I told him to go to the Devil. I can't wait to rid my hands of this nasty business and of him.

Was this proof of Colonel Morrell really doing something illegal? And was Alice's safety being threatened while she was in Iraq? Perhaps

Colonel Morrell wasn't trying to save Bosworth Manor, but his daughter.

Mona remembered Morrell as being overprotective. He insisted both Alice and Mona take guards with them every time they ventured outside the compound. Discovering she had more to fear from a violent British officer than from the local people, Mona moved into the village and bought a gun from one of the black market runners. It was only when outside agitators began poisoning the minds of the locals, did Mona decide to leave the region, taking Alice with her.

Looking at her watch, Mona saw that it was half past noon. Where had the time gone? She locked the secret room and pulled back the drapes. Upon leaving the study, she heard Alice and Farley talking outside the front door and decided to join them. She found Alice sitting behind the wheel of a maroon and crème colored, Duesenberg convertible with Farley sitting in the back seat.

Mona laughed at Farley's visual joke. "So this is your rental? Looks like she could fly down the road."

"Isn't she a beauty!" Farley cried, jumping out

and sweeping open the front passenger door for Mona.

Alice giggled while fiddling with the car's knobs and controls. "We must take it for a spin."

"It will have to wait. Lunch awaits us," Mona said.

"After lunch then," Alice insisted. "Robert?"

"We can take it out later this afternoon."

"Promise?"

"Of course, Alice. I've never seen you so excited by a car before."

"I love it. Everything about it is so sleek. So elegant. My Rolls is on its last legs."

Mona teased, "Alice, if I didn't know better, I'd say you were falling in love with this car."

"At least a car can't betray you," Alice said, bitterly.

Farley's smile faded at her remark, and he stormed inside the manor.

Mona put her hand on Alice's shoulder. "Alice, I don't know what happened between you and Farley, but he traveled all the way from Kentucky to help you. Give him a little leeway, will ya? It's not like you to be unkind, at least, not the Alice I know."

"You knew a young girl who had never known anything but happiness, then boom, the roof caves in, and that young girl didn't have the resources to deal with the loss. I'm not a silly girl anymore, but I'm afraid the grown-up Alice is not coping very well either, Mona."

"Farley and I will do our best to help you."

"What do you know about Robert?"

"Not much, but he seems to be a caring person if a little unorthodox."

"I grew up with Robert, but I haven't had contact with him for years."

"Why?"

"One day I will tell you what happened between us, but right now, let's have some lunch."

Thinking Alice was ducking the issue, Mona said, "I'm going to hold you to that promise, Alice."

Before going inside, Mona and Alice positioned the roof back on the car and rolled up its windows, as it looked like it was going to rain and then scurried inside as the first droplets hit the ground.

Mona followed Alice to the dining hall thinking she was going to get to the bottom of Alice's discord with Farley, but questioned her intention.

Did she really want to know about Farley and Alice?

Did she really?

8

Mona unfolded her napkin as George served Yorkshire pudding with bangers and mash.

"What's this?" Alice asked.

"Compliments of His Lordship and Miss Mona, Lady Alice."

Farley remarked, "It looks delicious."

"George, was Violet moved?" Mona asked.

"The room was ready when she returned from the village."

"What's this? Who's moved?"

Mona addressed Alice. "I told George to move Violet next to me."

"Without asking me?"

"I was under the impression the butler took care of the household issues and not the lord or lady."

Farley said, "Quite right. What are you stirred up about, Alice?"

Alice shook her head. "I don't know what I am doing or what is going on around me anymore. So sorry."

Farley shot Mona an odd look before cutting into his Yorkshire pudding.

Eager to change the subject, Mona asked, "How did the accounting books look?"

"They were in better shape than expected," Farley said. "It's true the estate is down on its luck, but it has many assets in tenant homes and farm equipment. I'm confident the bank will listen to reason."

"I brought these assets to the bank's attention previously, Robert," Alice said.

"I can be more persuasive," Farley reiterated.

"Let's hope so," Mona said, motioning to George to fill her water glass.

"What about your morning, Mona?"

Ignoring Alice, Mona asked, "Farley, are we still going to have a drive after lunch?"

"If it stops raining."

"I'm game if you and Alice are." Mona speared a bite of food with her fork, placing her left hand in her lap while Alice and Farley held a knife and fork in both hands.

"I thought we were going to the bank, Robert."

"We can go tomorrow morning. Will you be free?"

"Right after breakfast then." Alice turned to Mona. "You still haven't told us about your morning."

"I'll tell you later," Mona said, motioning with her head toward George.

Alice understood Mona's signal and concentrated on her food. "This is quite lovely," she said cutting into a large sausage the British called a banger. "I haven't had bangers and mash for such a long time."

"Who doesn't like mashed potatoes with onion gravy? My absolute favorite," Mona declared.

Realizing Mona didn't want to speak in front of George, Farley ate with relish not adding much to the conversation. He took the time to reflect upon the bank meeting tomorrow. Although he had reassured Alice, Farley was not confident about the outcome of his negotiations with them. To be sure the note on Bosworth Manor had too high an interest rate on it. The question was would the bank listen to reason about lowering the rate? Farley felt the bank was deliberately trying to cast Alice into penury as the land was extremely valuable. Banks were known to look to the future, and a rising British population would need housing and land to build the housing upon. Farley put his worries aside as he would find out tomorrow if Alice's bank was on the up and up or trying to swindle her. At the moment, he meant to enjoy his meal, and by golly, he was going to savor it. He hadn't had bangers and mash for years. He had learned to enjoy American Southern cooking, but he missed the food of his birthplace—jolly England.

Farley might well admit it.

He missed England.

9

Farley let Alice drive the Duesenberg to an abandoned farmhouse on the estate. It was obvious Alice loved the car, but they were on a mission. Mona had something to say to them both, which she didn't want the servants to overhear. He was curious as to the nature of Mona's report.

After Alice parked the car, Farley unlocked the farmhouse door, which squeaked and moaned as he pushed it open.

"This is old Tom Mullin's cottage. He died last year, and I've never been able to replace him. We'll be able to talk in private here," Alice said.

The cottage was basically one room with a bed and bathroom off to the side. Mona sat at a large harvest table in the kitchen and pulled the journal from a canvas bag she had brought, laying it on the table.

"What's that?" Farley asked.

"Ask Alice."

"Alice?"

"I see you've found my father's journal. I should have known you would. You're such a clever girl."

"What's she talking about?" Farley asked Mona.

"I'm afraid Alice knows more than she's letting on."

"I don't understand."

"I found this journal in a secret panel on the side of the desk. I haven't read all of it, but what I have read supports my suspicions about Alice's father smuggling artifacts out of Iraq." Mona directed her next remark to Alice. "I suppose you have read all of it."

"Yes, I have."

"So you have some idea of who is sending you those letters?"

"As you do as well, Mona."

Farley looked between the two women facing each other across the large plank table. "Who is it?"

Mona turned to Farley. "Colonel Morrell was indeed smuggling artifacts because he was pressured by M. S. to do so."

"Who is M. S.?"

Mona answered, "There are two possible suspects. One is Mohammed al-Sharif. He was the leader of a tribe living near the village where we were stationed in Iraq. He had his thumb in every black market scheme. Looting for antiquities was big business and helped fund his rise to power. To cover his tracks, he preached against the British, saying they were stealing artifacts. Another is Marden Sinclair, a British soldier. He was a young lieutenant under Colonel Morrell's command."

"Why do you suspect a British soldier?"

Alice hesitated for a moment, but then said, "Because he attacked Mona."

"What do you mean by 'attacked?'"

"You know what is meant. If it hadn't been for Alice hearing my cries and rushing in when she did, my corpse would have been found in the desert. There was no way Sinclair would have let me live after he abused me."

"The filthy badger!" Farley cried. "Alice, did

he ever touch you?"

"Sinclair was obsessed with Mona, but even if his attention had been focused on me, I was a woman with a title. He never would have dared look my way, but Mona was alone and an American who wore pants, working at a traditional man's job. She was fair game."

Mona added, "Sinclair hated me because I had rebuffed him several times, and he decided to teach me a lesson. Alice picked up a shovel and hit him over the head. We both escaped."

"Did you report this . . . this Sinclair?"

"Alice and I went directly to Colonel Morrell and told him what happened. Colonel Morrell said he was not going to ruin a young man's life because a little kissy face got out of hand."

"I don't believe it. Colonel Morrell would never have acted so unseemly. That is not the man I knew."

Alice said, "It's true, Robert. I was present when he said so to Mona. I was shocked as well."

"That's when I moved into the village and bought a gun. Sinclair had carte blanche to do as he willed with me because Colonel Morrell was not going to punish him."

"I thought I knew the man. I can't believe Colonel Morrell would ignore such a breach of military discipline and especially from one of his own men." Farley seemed genuinely distressed.

Alice and Mona waited patiently until he collected himself.

Finally, Farley asked, "What happened to these two men?"

"Sinclair was reportedly killed during the attack, and al-Sharif became a prominent leader in Iraq after the British left."

"I still don't see why the subterfuge, Alice. What does this journal have to do with what's going on now?"

Mona interrupted, "I think I was brought here as bait, and you were summoned to act as my protector. Isn't that correct, Alice? You think Marden Sinclair is still alive and sending you those letters."

Alice glanced timidly down at her folded hands, but then spoke boldly. "Yes. I knew you would find Father's journal, Mona, and that you would put some of the pieces together."

"You lied to us, Alice," Farley accused, stunned.

"No, I didn't, Robert. I asked for help. I showed you the letters. I had my suspicions, but I wasn't sure. I didn't want to predispose your thinking. I needed a fresh approach to see if you both came to the same conclusion."

"You put me in danger," Mona said.

"The letters are to me. They threaten me. Not you." Alice said heatedly. "My house was broken into. My dog killed. My man hurt."

"Okay, but you should have been up front, especially about a man who tried to ravage Mona possibly lurking nearby."

Mona said, "Tell us why you think these events are happening."

"I think Father was pressured into supplying artifacts to Marden Sinclair to sell on the black market."

Farley opened the journal and skimmed the last entries. "How could Sinclair put pressure on your father?"

"Sinclair was a most unscrupulous man. There were rumors he traded in the flesh pot markets as well. I think he threatened Father with my abduction. He states as much in his journal. That's why Father was so insistent that Mona and

I have guards with us at all times, but we were both so naïve and headstrong, we didn't heed him."

Mona added, "I thought he was trying to control us. The hubris of the very young. I feel so foolish now."

Farley asked, "Why didn't your father have Sinclair arrested and court-martialed?"

"I wondered about that myself. I've come to the conclusion Sinclair didn't work alone. He may have been working with other men in Father's brigade and with al-Sharif as well. Perhaps Father didn't know whom to trust and worried about a mutiny," Alice suggested.

"You think there was a network of British and Iraqis together working the black market?"

Alice said, "Yes, I do, Mona. I think they were peddling in both antiquities and female flesh."

"But why bother you now?"

"I think Father took something from them. Something very valuable."

"How did you get your father's journal, Alice?" Farley inquired, closing the volume.

"It was sent back to England along with his body and other personal effects."

"His body? You mean he wasn't buried in Iraq?" Farley asked, wondering how the body could have been preserved.

"Father requested that his body be shipped back to England in any event of his demise overseas."

"Where is he buried?"

"In the family's mausoleum on the estate."

Mona asked, "Did you view the body?"

"Lord, no. It would have had considerable damage. I didn't want to see Father in such a ravished state."

Mona put the journal back in the canvas bag. "Did anyone view the body?"

"He came in a simple wooden box. I had the local carpenter build a large casket, and he inserted the box into the casket for me. The body was delivered during the winter, so I had the box stored in one of the barns until the casket was ready."

"How long after I left for the States did your father's body arrive?"

"A month later. Mona, why are you asking about Father's remains?"

"I'm just trying to get a timeline of events.

Did anyone from his unit contact you?"

"I received very little information about my father's death. I was mailed a brief report of the attack and a list of the men who died with him. Sinclair's name was on the list as one of the dead."

Mona requested, "I'd like to see the report."

"Surely."

Farley lit a cigarette and crushed the burning match with his shoe. "Why do you think Sinclair is still alive?"

"From the message scrawled on my mirror. The letters were typed, but the lipstick message was written in cursive. The Y was embellished with many decorative loops. The only person I've known to make such a Y was Marden Sinclair. I think he faked his death and has been working as an agent for al-Sharif ever since. It was al-Sharif who orchestrated the attack at my father's compound."

"This is a matter for MI6," Farley announced decisively.

"And what would I tell them, Robert? I think Sinclair is alive because I saw a Y on my mirror that looked like a dead man's Ys? I think foreign agents are after me because my father stole something of value from their sovereign nation? I have no proof of any of this, and I don't want my father's name dragged through the mud if true. Fleet Street loves to dig its bloody claws into who's left of the aristocracy. We are treated like the plague in the press."

"And with good reason," Farley replied.

"Oh, Robert, you were always fighting your birthright. What don't you accept who you are?"

"And who is that?" Mona asked, disturbed at how the discussion was becoming personal.

"Don't you know, Mona? Robert is to be Duke of Brynelleth when his father passes. He is the Marquess of Gower, ninth in line to become king of the British Empire. He is of the *blood royale!*"

10

Mona reached over the table and slapped Farley's face.

"Is that any way to treat a future king of England?" Farley said sardonically, rubbing his cheek, but he was speaking to air as Mona had rushed out of the farmhouse.

"Mona certainly has a bee in her bonnet. What's up with her?" a bewildered Farley asked Alice.

"Oh, Robert. Can't you see Mona is falling in love with you?"

"She is?"

"Really! Sometimes you are so stupid."

"What do you think about that?" Robert said to no one in particular watching through a dirty window as Mona hurried down a pathway.

"What are you going to do about it?"

"Nothing at the moment. I am here to help you out of this nasty business, so you are my first priority. I'll deal with Mona later."

"Don't hurt her, Robert. Don't hurt her like you did me."

"If I recall, it was you who called things off between us. I never wanted to break our engagement."

Alice looked wounded. "You made things so difficult. I had no choice."

"The bloody hell you didn't," Farley said, his voice rising from anger. "We're done here. Get in the car. I'm taking you home. Tomorrow I'll fix things at the bank. We'll find out who is harassing you, and then I'm going back to Kentucky where I have peace."

"Are you going to speak with Mona about us?"

"Not unless she asks me. Have you told her about us?"

"No, but I think I should."

"I wish you wouldn't. Let the past be in the past. There's nothing between us now."

"How do you feel about her?"
"Let it go, lass. Let it go."
But Alice felt she couldn't.

11

Robert Farley was reading the evening paper with a whisky before a cheerful fire when Mona stuck her head in the library.

"May I come in?" she asked.

"As long as you don't plan to slap me again."

Mona entered wearing a beaded black and blue kimono over a pale blue slipper dress and took a seat next to Farley. "About that. I'm truly sorry. I don't know what possessed me. I'm so ashamed."

"It seems when you are surprised, you strike out. Remember when you struck me at the ball?"

"You popped out of nowhere. How was I to know if you were friend or foe?"

"After learning what happened to you in Iraq, I see why you react as you do when caught off guard. And yet you went back to Iraq for a second time."

"I needed a job, and the locals never bothered me. I asked for protection from the local imam and received his blessing for the work I was doing because he thought it important. Remember Gertrude Bell had only died in 1926. These people had great respect for her and she was a cartographer as well, so they passed that respect on to me."

"You're an interesting woman, Mona. Gutsy."

"Do you forgive me?"

"Does it matter if I forgive you?"

"Well, we are neighbors, and I don't want there to be any bad blood between us."

"Would you really like to tell me why you were so startled?"

"It was a shock, that's all. You've been parading around Kentucky as Bobby Farley, a minor lord from somewhere in England, horse breeder, and ne'er-do-well. Then I find out you're some grand duke of royal blood no less."

"I never lied about being a peer of the realm. I just didn't let on how high up on the food chain I was. Americans have a notorious distaste for the

European ruling class and all that goes with it. However, a run of the mill lord is a dime a dozen as far as Americans are concerned. Farley is my legal name, but Lord Farley is not the correct title. It is Lord Gower, but such distinctions only cause confusion. I just simplified things for the American mindset and was trying to fit in Kentucky as you were in Iraq. If it would make you feel any better, I'm no longer considered a royal since 1917. King George V fixed that. My father is just a regular duke now, much to his chagrin."

"Are you still in line to the throne?"

"If everyone else croaks."

"Always a lovely thought with you."

"There's my sarcastic cow. A scrapper till the end."

Mona's eyes widened in surprise. "I did it again, didn't I? I don't know why, but you bring out the worst in me."

"You look especially exquisite tonight. The moisture in the English air has brought a rose hue to your skin and your hair glows like a luminous halo."

Mona blushed. "Thank you."

"Now tell me. How do you dye your hair so white?"

"Her hair color is natural," Alice said striding in the library and bending over to kiss Mona on the cheek. "I can attest to it."

Farley chuckled.

Mona looked furious. "He knows my hair is natural."

"Ignore Robert when he tries to get your goat, dear. I do."

"I think I need a drink. Do you want one, Alice?" Mona asked, as she went over to the bar and poured a glass of vodka.

"I'll take a sherry, dear. Do you think Roosevelt will end Prohibition in the States?" Alice asked, reaching for the drink Mona poured for her.

"I think Roosevelt shall end it. He promised."

"I hope so," Robert said. "Everyone needs a stiff belt over there to take their minds off the horrible economy. Even with all my resources, I'm only keeping my head above water. How's Moon Enterprises doing?"

Mona replied, "There is a high demand for copper, so we shall see record profits this year and the next, especially with all the new building projects announced by the government. All those buildings need copper plumbing."

"I like being around any woman who can support me in a grand style."

"How was your walk back, Mona?" Alice asked, ignoring Farley's last comment.

"It reminded me of the long walks Elizabeth Bennett took in *Pride and Prejudice*. It gave me time to think."

"About?"

"Alice, how many priest holes are in this house? Catholic houses usually built more than one, and are there any secret passageways leading from one bedroom to another?"

"There is another secret chamber on the first floor in the great hall. A secret door in the back of my closet leads to passageways throughout the manor. It seems the former Morrells used them for their love lives when they had guests."

"Where do the passageways lead other than the bedrooms?"

"It's been so long since I've been in one I don't recall."

Farley spoke up. "They lead to a subterranean

tunnel downstairs and out through the garden to an exit point near the stables. The Morrells intended to use it as a point of escape in case agents of Elizabeth I caught them practicing the Catholic faith."

"My brother and I used to scare the servants by popping out suddenly and crying boo. You know how cruel children can be."

Mona asked, "So George and other servants may be aware of the passageways?"

"Yes."

"Would they be aware of the priest holes?"

"I don't think so. I never knew about them until I reached twenty-one. Father showed me both rooms on a Sunday after the servants had gone to church. He told me never to tell anyone of their existence."

"Yesterday I thought I saw someone in the upstairs hallway when coming down to dinner."

"It may have been a maid turning down the beds."

"I called out and asked them to identify themselves, but no one responded. If Marden Sinclair is alive as you believe, he may be using the tunnel to get into the house."

"He can't. The tunnel is locked by an iron gate."

Refreshing Alice's sherry, Farley asked, "When was the last time you checked the gate?"

"Last year maybe."

Farley said, "If it was Marden Sinclair who attacked your man Jansen, he may have come through the old tunnel into the house."

"I shan't sleep a wink tonight. I haven't thought about those old passageways in years, but it makes sense."

"We need to search the house and make sure Bosworth Manor can't be breached from the tunnel," Mona suggested.

"We'll do it tomorrow when we can see properly in daylight," Farley said.

"What about tonight?" Alice asked.

"I think you ladies should bunk together tonight, and I'll sleep in the adjoining maid's room. Mona, have Violet join you as well."

Mona said, "One of us should keep watch while the others sleep. Even you, Farley. You can't stay up all night."

"We'll worry about such matters later. Let's keep our chins up, not letting the servants notice we're concerned. After all, one of them may be helping Marden Sinclair. If he is alive, we don't want him to be tipped off."

"I refuse to believe such a thing. The remaining servants have been with this household for ages."

"When's the last time you paid their wages?"

"It's been months I'm afraid."

Farley and Mona didn't speak as they let Alice's words sink in.

Realizing the enormity of her statement, Alice said softly, "Oh, I see what you mean. You think one of them might be receiving money to let the intruder in."

"Don't worry, Alice. We'll get your finances straightened out tomorrow at the bank, but let's get through this evening first. We'll have a nice dinner, play some card games, and go to bed. Everything will look better in the morning."

Alice shot Farley a grateful look.

Humiliated, Mona pushed away feelings of jealousy. She had no right to feel the way she did. Mona didn't even like Farley, but she had come to rely on him. And even if she had come to care for him, how could she compete with Alice's patrician good looks, raven hair, and startling blue eyes? She was the type of woman Farley needed in a wife—breeding, brains, and a title. Alice was one of the *swells*.

She didn't have long to ponder on her battered emotional state as George announced dinner was ready. Mona decided she would see this mission through with Alice and then she was going home with Violet, never to look back.

12

"Are we in danger?"

"It's a precaution just for tonight, Violet, until we can search the house tomorrow. Lord Farley will be in the connecting bedroom with the door opened."

"You mean Lord Farley might see me in my nightshift?"

"You don't have anything that Lord Farley hasn't seen before. Wear something loose and comfortable. I'm wearing my daytime lounging pajamas."

"I have a cotton pair of pj's."

"Now that we've got your attire for the night settled, I want you to do something tomorrow. How are you getting along with young Danny?"

"We're hitting it off," Violet replied, grinning.

"I think Danny has taken a liking to me."

"Good. Tomorrow I want you to have Danny boy take you to the pub in the village. There is a man by the name of Jansen working there. He was attacked in Bosworth Manor."

"One of the maids told me about the incident."

"Chat him up, Violet. See if he has anything to say about the attack or working at Bosworth Manor."

"How am I to do that?"

"I understand he's thirty or so and unmarried. You're a young pretty thing. Use your feminine wiles to get him talking."

"How?"

"It's easy with a man. Smile a lot, laugh at his jokes, and act as though you're interested in his patois, no matter how boring."

"I'll do my best."

"That's all I ask of you. Get Danny talking as well. A couple of pints of the pub's ale might loosen both their tongues."

"I'll have Danny take me into the village on the pretext of having more of Lady Alice's shoes repaired. We can wait at the pub while they are being repaired."

"Excellent. How is our little project coming along?"

"Oh, Miss, it's sad to see fine garments reduced to such a state. Even her lingerie is tattered. I'm doing the best I can, but I feel dreadful sneaking about her room. It's unseemly."

"It would shame Lady Alice to confront her with the state of her clothing. Subterfuge is the best way to handle this. How far along are you?"

"I've gone through the two chests of drawers mending her underthings and lingerie. I fixed the rip in her favorite sweater, mended the linings on all her coats, and repaired most of her shoes. I'll start going through her day frocks and evening dresses tomorrow."

"She and Lord Farley are going to the bank tomorrow morning. You'll have several hours after they leave to make some headway."

"I'll need a sewing machine for alterations, Miss."

"Does Bosworth Manor have a sewing machine?"

"There is a nice one in the laundry room—a Singer with foot pedals. Just like the one my mother taught me on."

"If the other servants question its use, tell them Lady Alice asked you to put right a few of her things. I doubt they will mention it to her."

"Yes, Miss."

"As soon as you are ready, we'll go to Lady Alice's suite. She has a fainting couch made up for you. I'll bunk in her bed."

"If you insist, Miss."

"It will do for tonight. Err on the side of caution I always say."

"The maid whose room I shared said the ghosts of Bosworth Manor had been restless of late."

"In what way?"

"Unusual noises at night like tapping on the walls. Things in disarray in the morning such as desk drawers pulled out or doors left open."

"Hmm."

"Do you think ghosts are roaming the hallways, Miss?"

"I haven't heard anything. Have you?"

"Nothing, and I'm a light sleeper."

Mona laughed but stopped when Violet looked askance at her. She knew for a fact that

Violet was a heavy sleeper, and nothing, short of a bomb, would wake her. However, Violet was always up at six, making ready for the day.

"I'm going to Lady Alice's room," Mona said when part of a wall suddenly pushed open.

Violet screamed as Mona reached for her gun.

Lady Alice peeked around the hidden door, holding a flashlight. "It's only me. Don't shoot."

"Lordy, you gave me a fright," Mona complained.

"I don't want the servants to know you are sleeping in my room. This is the best way. Come on." Alice said, waving them into the hidden corridor.

Mona and Violet stepped tentatively into a narrow hallway, looking about before following Lady Alice.

"It looks awfully clean," Violet remarked.

Alice motioned them into her room. "I have the servants sweep them out and set rat traps throughout the year."

"So everyone in the village knows about these corridors," Mona said.

"I told you my brother and I would pop out at the servants. Besides, why keep them a secret? All these old homes have such passageways. Versailles even gives tours of its secret corridors."

"Who is Versailles?" Violet asked.

Mona answered, "Not a who, but a what. It's a magnificent palace in France."

"Oh," Violet said, wishing she hadn't asked. It made her appear uneducated.

Lady Alice closed the hidden door.

"You can't even tell a door is there, Miss!" Violet exclaimed.

Mona had to agree the door was marvelous workmanship.

"Make yourselves at home. Robert thought to sneak some food up from the kitchen. Might be a long night."

"It might indeed," Farley said walking from the maid's room, shaking a glass pitcher. "Martinis, anyone?"

"This late at night?" Alice groused.

"It's never too late, my dear," Farley said, pouring himself a drink.

Violet immediately went over to Lady Alice's desk where food was laden and picked up two chocolate bonbons.

Farley chortled. "Imagine my surprise when I sneaked into the kitchen and found three boxes of candy."

"I told Violet to purchase some sweets for the staff."

"And Violet likes chocolate bonbons," Farley added.

Violet confessed, "I have a sweet tooth."

Alice helped herself to several bonbons while Mona made a butter sandwich and peeled an orange.

While everyone was having their late snack, Mona asked, "Alice, after the break-in, did you have servants patrol at night?"

"I couldn't ask them to do more than what they were doing, and I didn't have money in the budget to hire a guard."

"One of the maids told Violet that the ghosts of the Manor were stirring, saying they were hearing strange noises and finding things out of place in the morning. Did the servants report this to you?"

Alice looked surprised. "No, they didn't. I know nothing about this. Of course, the under servants would have reported to George, and he reports directly to me."

"Would George have mentioned this to you?"

"Not if he didn't think it had any validity. As butler, he is in charge of running the household.

George rarely discusses such matters with me."

Intrigued, Violet asked, "If I may be so bold as to ask, what does he discuss with you?"

Shocked that a maid would speak to her without being addressed first, Alice soldiered on. After all, Violet was an American with the appalling notion of equality. "Approval for the menus. If I'm to have guests for the weekend or if I'll be needing the car for the day. That type of thing," she replied without looking at Violet.

Mona bit her lip noticing Alice's reluctance to address Violet directly. Although annoyed by the snobbish attitude of the British upper-class toward their "inferiors," this was no time to give Alice a lecture that the world had changed, and Alice had better change with it.

Violet looked questioningly at Mona, "Did I say something wrong?"

Mona teased, "You just upset a hundred years of Victorian stuffiness, Violet."

Farley swallowed his martini before asking, "How many servants sleep in the house still?"

"George, of course. Danny and two house-maids."

"That's all?" Farley asked, astounded how small the live-in staff was for Bosworth Manor.

"We no longer have a housekeeper, but four women from the village come in twice a month to clean. The cook and her staff come to work at eight and leave after seven. It's up to George and two lads-in-waiting to serve the meals."

"What do the housemaids do?"

"They are poor girls from the village. They set the fires in the rooms and clean the grates when needed. They help wherever needed and get a jump on washing the dinner dishes after George brings them down."

"You have no scullery maid?"

"When George can acquire them. Young girls don't want to work in service anymore. They want employment in shops or factories where they can make more money and have more free time."

"So it seems only George, Danny, and two maids are sleeping in this house tonight besides us. A total of eight people. That's a small number of people for so large a house. Lot of ground to cover," Mona said.

"Let's get some sleep. I'll take the first watch," Farley suggested. "Mona, I'll wake you up at two."

"Fine with me."

Alice said, "Goodnight, Robert."

"Goodnight, ladies," Farley said, before stepping into the maid's room.

Mona laid her pistol on the nightstand and turned on the small light in the bathroom. "Violet, are you settled?"

"Yes, Miss."

"Do you need anything? An extra pillow?"

"I'm fine, Miss."

Mona climbed into bed with Alice. "I'm switching off the main lights then."

When neither Alice nor Violet responded, Mona turned off the lamp on her bedstead as did Alice with the lamp on her side.

The first to fall asleep was Violet whose rhythmic snoring allowed Mona to drift off only to have troubled dreams where she heard Farley call her name but she couldn't reach him in a dense fog.

"Mona. Mona! Wake up."

Jerking awake, Mona opened her eyes to see Farley peering down at her.

"Get up, woman, and grab your gun. Someone is about!"

13

Mona shot out of bed.

Alice stirred. "What is it?"

"Someone is in the hallway."

Farley said, "Mona, come with me."

"It's probably George," Alice said.

"At this hour of the night?" Mona questioned.

"Alice, you and Violet stay here."

"I don't think you have to worry about Violet," Mona claimed, checking on her maid. "I told you that girl could sleep through a tornado."

Farley pulled open the hidden door. "We'll go out through one of the other bedrooms. Alice, pull a chest across the entrance when we close this door so no one can enter."

"Be careful. Both of you." Jumping from her bed, Alice waited until Mona and Farley disappeared into the maw of the sinister corridor and silently closed the door before dragging a chest across the secret entrance. Fearful, she placed a chair under the door locks of her suite. Wide awake, Alice sat in a chair near the fire, jumping at every little sound. The wind rattled the panes in the window and caused the ancient copper gutters to groan, scraping the brick façade. A solitary mantel clock sounded menacing as it counted off the seconds. Even the soft snoring of Violet worked to shatter Alice's nerves.

Would this night never be over?

14

Farley and Mona traversed the corridor until they came to Mona's room and slipped through the false door. Mona followed only to bump into some furniture.

"Be quiet," Farley ordered.

"It's hard to see without a flashlight."

"Shh. Hear that?"

"Let's move. We can catch him in the act."

Farley quietly opened the door to the hallway and poked his head around the door jamb. "Look there," he whispered, pointing.

Down at the other end of the hallway, a single light moved in the darkness.

Mona stepped out from behind Farley and pointed her gun. "Stop. I have the drop on you!"

A flashlight came hurling at Farley and Mona

who ducked thinking she was going to be struck.

Falling short of them, the flashlight cast eerie shadows on the wall. Farley ran and picked it up while Mona found the hall light switch. They both shielded their faces until their eyes adjusted to the hall light.

"What's going on?" George demanded, pushing through a door that guarded the servants' stairway. He stood angrily with disarrayed hair and wearing a thick robe over his pajamas.

"Did you come from the third floor?" Farley asked.

"I heard shouting and a thump. Woke me up."

"He must be downstairs then," Mona said. "George, wake up Danny and help us search the downstairs. Someone is in the house."

"Can't be. I locked up myself," George argued.

Mona didn't wait but pushed through the doorway to the servants' stairs and hurried down the stone steps.

Farley followed close behind crying out, "Mona, wait."

Upon reaching the first floor, Mona found

herself in the great hall. Farley was behind her and turned on the lights.

"Listen," Mona cautioned.

"Nothing," Farley said. "He could be anywhere. I'm calling the police."

"And tell them what? How are you going to explain all of us were in Lady Alice's bedroom? I see how that would be played out in the village. They'll say we were engaged in an orgy."

"My mouth waters at the thought."

"Be serious."

"I am."

"He's got to be here or in the basement."

"The intruder could be outside for all we know."

An out-of-breath George and an excited Danny brandishing an antique sword he had pulled off a wall joined Farley and Mona.

"What do you plan to do with that sword? Give someone tetanus?" Farley asked Danny.

"Better than nothing, sir."

"Shall I get the shotguns out of the trophy room?" George asked.

"No time for that. You two check the windows and doors. Miss Mona and I will inspect outside."

"Very good. I'll see to it immediately."

Farley and Mona hurried outside and searched the grounds around Bosworth Manor finding nothing. Disappointed, they returned to the house to find Alice had come downstairs along with the frightened maids.

Farley advised the servants to go to their rooms. "Sunrise is in a few hours. Let's get some sleep, shall we? We'll take this up later today. Danny, please escort the ladies back to the third floor. I'll see Lady Alice and Miss Mona to their rooms."

One of the maids, who broke into tears, calmed down when Lady Alice offered her a handkerchief.

"Please take it," Alice said. "I'm so sorry your rest was disturbed. Please do as Lord Farley asks. Go back to bed. George, you look exhausted. Breakfast shall be an hour later to give everyone extra sleep. I'll leave a note for cook."

"I'll do it," Mona offered. Still holding her gun, Mona made her way to the kitchen. Finding the cook's desk, she left a note about breakfast. Hearing footsteps on the stairway, Mona swung around holding her gun out.

Farley entered the kitchen and held up his hands. "Whoa, there, partner."

Mona put the gun in her pocket. "Checking up on me?"

"Alice has gone up with the rest. I wanted to escort you back to her room."

"I think the excitement is over for the night, so I'll go back my room. Violet can stay where she is for the night."

Farley appraised Mona. "Your hair is messy. It's sticking straight up in the back."

"Do you never stop criticizing me?" Mona complained, brushing past him.

Farley grabbed Mona's arm and pulled her to him. Holding her tightly, Farley kissed Mona passionately.

Mona responded with a fervor she had never experienced before with a man. A heated sensation rose from her belly to her lips, making her feel lightheaded. Instead of pulling away, Mona wrapped her arms around Farley inhaling his scent of tobacco, shaving cologne, and pomade.

Farley picked Mona up and pushed her against a wall, kissing her hair, temples, and the inside of her wrists before returning to her lips.

Mona returned his kisses with the same ardor until she heard—"Mona, are you coming to bed?"

Both Farley and Mona looked up to see Alice watching them with a contorted expression on her face.

"Alice," Mona blurted out, feeling angry with Alice for interrupting them.

Gently, Farley put Mona down and shot Alice a dark look.

"You didn't come back upstairs, so I came to look for you."

Confused at the quick turn of events, Mona took a moment to collect herself until she realized her moment with Farley was over. "Coming, Alice." Mona turned to Farley. "Goodnight."

"Robert?"

"I'm going to have another look around before I turn in. Goodnight," he replied gruffly, more to Alice than to Mona.

Mona reluctantly followed Alice. She paused long enough to glimpse Farley standing at the bottom of the servants' stairs and watching the two women ascend.

Farley smiled and nodded.

Mona returned his smile before continuing to climb up the staircase, wondering why Alice had acted so. If she had caught Farley and Alice kissing, she would have done the polite thing and discreetly left. Mona realized she would have been angry, but she would have let them have their moment together. And why would she have been angry to see Farley kiss Alice? Was she falling in love with Lawrence Robert Emerton Dagobert Farley? Mona hoped it was lust rather than love. Being in love with Farley meant only heartache. Her life was in Kentucky, and Farley's future was in England. The two were incompatible.

Was that why Alice had been so intent on stopping them?

Was it to protect Mona?

Or was it something else?

15

"I'm going to spend the rest of the night in my room, if you don't mind."

"I can see you are angry with me, Mona. Please come into my room and allow me to explain."

"I don't want to discuss Farley."

"Please, Mona. I want to share something with you."

"If you insist, but make it quick. I'm exhausted." Mona followed Alice into the bedroom.

Violet was still lightly snoring, dead to the world, and ignorant of the night's events.

Alice unlocked a box on her vanity and took out a picture. "Here," she said, handing Mona a picture. It was of Alice and Farley smiling at each other and holding hands. They looked young and fresh.

"That was us in 1917. Robert had been called for service as he had turned 18, so we decided to get married. This is our engagement picture."

Mona gazed intently at the picture. "You both look very much in love."

Alice took back the picture and locked it away. "We were."

"What happened?"

Alice sighed. "The war happened. My brother's death knocked us both for a loop, but we were young, so we recovered fast, thinking his death was the worst that could befall us." She paused, drifting off with her thoughts of the past.

"Alice?"

"The Robert who came back to me wasn't the Robert who had proposed to me. He had fought bravely, was awarded medals, but came back a broken man. Robert suffered from shellshock. After coming home, he locked himself in his room and wouldn't come out for months, rejecting contact with his father and me."

"Terrible."

"Yes, it was awful. Finally, Robert must have worked something out in his mind and emerged from his self-imposed exile. We tried to make it work, but his heart wasn't into getting married anymore. Robert traveled most of the time, and communication with him was sparse. In 1923, he came home and we tried again, but this time I was having doubts whether we could make a go of it. I thought that were his father to die, Robert wouldn't be able to cope with the responsibility of being duke. I broke it off with him in 1926 and joined my father in Mesopotamia."

"Where we met."

"Precisely. Robert left for Kentucky while I was gone."

"And you're telling me this because you don't think I'm the right woman for him."

"He's damaged goods, Mona."

"I'm damaged, too, Alice. Perhaps we'd make a good fit."

"He will need to marry one of his own kind."

"You have no claim on Farley. You gave him up years ago."

"Do you really think you can play the part of a grand duchess?"

"It's true what people say about the nastiness of the British aristocracy."

"Robert's had affairs before. He's just passing

time with you."

"Wow, Alice. You are really outdoing yourself for witch of the year award. I'll help you get back on your feet again, but consider my debt paid. Goodnight."

Mona hurried to her own room and cried herself to sleep.

16

Mona woke up late. She looked at her travel watch. "Ten!" she cried, wondering how she had slept so late.

And where was Violet?

She took a shower and dressed in dark slacks and a white cotton shirt. After putting on makeup, Mona went downstairs to find Alice and Farley had left for the bank.

"Breakfast is laid out in the dining hall, Miss Mona," George said, coming up behind her.

"When did Lady Alice leave?"

"She left with Lord Gower a half hour ago."

Mona gave a ghost of a smile upon hearing George address Farley as Lord Gower. "Thank you, George." She went into the dining hall and found Violet eating.

"Violet, you're not supposed to be in here."

"I don't care. I'm not eating downstairs anymore. The other girls are mean to me."

Sighing, Mona fell into a chair and unfolded a napkin. "You're telling me."

"Something wrong, Miss?"

"No. Let's get some food into our bellies. We have a long day ahead of us."

Mona and Violet ate in silence until George entered carrying a pitcher of orange juice, which he almost dropped upon seeing Violet sitting at the mistress' table.

"My word!" he uttered.

Mona waved him away. "I asked Violet to have breakfast with me. We have details to go over, and this was the most convenient time to do so before Lady Alice and Lord Gower return."

"Who's Lord Gower?" Violet asked.

George's eyes widened at the obliviousness of Violet's question.

"It's all right, George. You may put the pitcher down on the table and leave."

"Very good, Miss."

"Who is Lord Gower?" Violet asked again.

"Switch subjects for now, Violet. How are the

repairs on Lady Alice's clothes coming?"

"Another day or so should be enough."

"Good. I want to wrap this up and leave."

Violet declared, "I miss home, too."

Mona nodded and ate in silence until Violet asked, "Anything happen last night?"

Mona gazed at Violet in surprise until she remembered Violet had slept undisturbed by the intruder. "Nothing for you to worry about."

Violet folded her napkin and announced. "I'm off to the village with Danny. Where will you be this afternoon?"

"I'll find you, Violet. Good luck with your sleuthing."

Violet giggled. "I feel like a regular Nancy Drew."

"Go out through the servants' entrance in the back, Violet. Otherwise George will have a stroke."

"I've got a bag with Lady Alice's shoes by the back door. Should be back to help with tea."

Mona slipped Violet a five pound note. "Be careful."

"I'll make you proud, Miss Mona. Don't fret." Violet left by the servants' corridor just as Mona heard George opening the front door for Lady Alice and Farley.

Farley asked if breakfast was still out, but Mona couldn't make out George's mumbled reply. Wanting to hear what the bank decided, Mona poured herself some coffee and waited.

A few minutes later, Alice and Farley both strolled in looking pleased.

"By the expression on both your faces, I trust the bank visit was a success."

"Robert was magnificent," Alice said, beaming at him.

"Mona, you would not believe how those scallywags were trying to cheat Alice. Disgraceful." Robert glanced at the buffet. "I'm glad breakfast is still out. I'm famished."

"No wonder after the fight you gave them. Oh, you should have seen Robert in action, Mona. He convinced the bank manager to lower my interest rate and extend the loan, or he would close down all of the Brynelleth accounts with the bank when he became duke."

Alice held up a wad of one pound notes. "Plus he got them to grant a small loan so I could pay the servants. What a glorious morning."

"Bully for you, Farley."

"Do I detect disapproval in your tone, Mona?" Farley questioned, spreading jam on a piece of toast.

"I'm very happy for you, Alice. Now let's concentrate on these threatening letters."

"Happily," Alice replied.

"If you will excuse me, I'm going to finish your father's journal today. Perhaps it can throw some light on the matter."

Alice cut into a salted kipper. "Whatever you think best, Mona."

"I'll think I'll skip lunch today. See you both at tea." She left the room leaving an astonished Farley gaping after her.

"Mona's awfully cold this morning. What did you say to her, Alice?"

"I told Mona about us."

"What else?"

"About the war and how you suffered from shellshock."

"Bloody hell, Alice. That is something I should have told her."

"Why didn't you?"

"I wasn't even sure Mona liked me. She's a

hard person to know."

"Maybe she sensed you weren't being honest with her."

"That is not something one discusses with another over tea."

"Perhaps you were never going to tell her."

"She stirs something inside me. I would like to explore it."

"In other words, she quickens you. A simple girl in the village can do that."

"I'm not talking about sex, Alice. Something deeper."

"She's American and a nobody without rank or title."

"That's a cruel thing to say about Mona. When you first met her, you took Mona under your wing as one might take in a shivering dog, but now she's more important than you. Mona is one of the richest women in the States. I think it bothers you."

"I'm happy for Mona."

"Are you?"

"It was Mona who got me out of Mesopotamia and home safely. She saved my life. Otherwise, I would have died with Father."

"As you saved her from Marden Sinclair. I would call it even between the two of you."

"Mona came because she loves me and wants to help. She doesn't owe me anything."

"Do you love her?"

"Of course, I do."

"Then leave us alone. We might have a chance for happiness if our affection for each other blooms."

"What about us? You know I'm the best candidate as a wife to you."

"That ship has sailed."

Alice put her arms around Farley. "Don't you remember how happy we were? We can be again."

Farley pulled away. "Alice, I will always love you. You are one of the dearest people to me, but I shall never marry you. There is too much sorrow in our past. When I look at you I see a constant reminder of paradise lost. The War took your brother. My brother died. As a result, both our mothers died of grief. We lost friends and comrades. It's too much. It may not be fair, but there it is."

"You are not reminded of the past with Mona."

"I see only the future with her."

"It isn't fair to me."

"I know, but you would never be happy with me. Find some other chap who doesn't carry so much baggage. He's out there, you know."

Alice acquiesced. She needed to accept that a future with Robert Farley was not in the cards for her.

But was he in the cards for Mona?

17

Violet entered the pub with Danny who was toting various packages for her. Danny waved at the bartender who nodded.

"Let's sit at this table."

"Can we sit at the bar?" Violet asked.

"There are no empty stools. This is a good table by the window."

Violet looked wistfully at the bartender chatting up a customer. The man fit the description Mona gave her for Jansen. She needed to talk with him, but how without being obvious?

"Yes, this is a nice table. I can watch the village square from here. I was wondering though if you could introduce me to some of your friends. I want the entire village experience."

"You can leave your purse and packages here.

No one will bother them. Come with me to order. I'll introduce you to Jansen. He used to work at Bosworth."

"How nice." Violet followed Danny to the bar, still holding her purse. She was not about to let it out of her sight, regardless of what Danny said. She had learned from Miss Mona not to trust anyone, especially men. Violet also remembered how Mona said to catch men's attention, so she smiled and looked pleasant.

"Violet, this is a mate of mine, Jansen. He used to work at Bosworth. Jansen, this is Violet."

Violet offered her hand. "Nice to meet you. I work for Mona Moon. She's here visiting Lady Alice."

"Lass, better lock your door at night. Strange goings on at that castle monstrosity. Danny boy here can tell you things that would make your hair curl," Jansen said, shaking Violet's hand.

"Bosworth seems like a lovely home."

"Ach, I myself was attacked by a ghost who killed Lady Alice's dog. Knocked me out, and when I awoke the poor thing was lying in a pool of blood, dead by my side."

"That's terrible!" Violet exclaimed. "Why do

you think it was a ghost and not an intruder?"

"Heard nothing. Saw nothing. It was like a spirit came out of the wall and attacked me."

Danny added, "Aye, Jansen's right. Strange things been going on. Noises in the middle of the night. Things moved about for no reason. Just last night, His Lordship and Miss Mona believed they saw an intruder and had the entire household searching the manor half of the night. George and I assisted, but we knew t'was but a spirit."

"How long have the spirits been active?" Violet asked, accepting a pint of ale from Jansen.

"Ever since the Master came home to rest," Jansen said.

"The Master?"

"Colonel Morrell," Danny stated. "But it was a year afterwards, wasn't it Jansen? He was laid to rest in January of 1929 and things didn't get squirrely until the summer of 1930. That's when we noticed odd things about the place."

"Was Lady Alice informed?"

Jansen and Danny looked questioningly at each other and shrugged.

"We have no contact with Lady Alice. George

is the employee who deals directly with Her Ladyship," Danny said.

Jansen added, "George might not have done so, as Lady Alice is known to be high strung."

"In what way?" Violet asked, putting down the heavy glass of beer.

Jansen looked both ways to see if anyone was listening and leaned forward in a confidential manner. "The lass drinks a bit more than she should and has crying fits."

A man at the other end of the bar overheard Jansen and said, "Is that any way to talk about your betters, man?"

Jansen scolded, "'Ow 'es Lady Alice any better 'n me? At least, I work for my supper. Mind your own business, mate. This is a private conversation."

Rebuffed, the gentleman grumbled at Jansen and took his beer to sit by the fire.

"This is such a fascinating story," Violet gushed, remembering Mona's advice to act interested. "Let's say this ghost was really an intruder. I've never heard of a ghost killing a dog and beating a man. Why do you think he was there? I mean the intruder, not the spirits."

"To steal, lass. He thought no one would be there, and when he stumbled across me and the Great Dane, he panicked."

"What did the thief take?"

"I can answer that, Violet," Danny said, trying to impress her with his inside knowledge of the theft. "Not much. A pearl necklace that needed to be restrung and a piece of costume jewelry. The only thing of value taken was the amethyst ring. It was Lady Alice's engagement ring from His Lordship. She wore it for years, even after he had departed for America."

"You mean Farley?" Violet gasped.

Danny looked surprised at Violet's reaction. "They were betrothed for years before Lady Alice broke it off. At least, that's what cook told me."

"I didn't know." Recovering quickly, Violet asked, "Was the ring valuable?"

"Aye," Jansen said, becoming suspicious of Violet's questions. "The amethyst was rare. The ring was Venetian, made in the seventeenth century."

Danny blabbed, "It was older than that, Jansen. I heard George describe it to the police after the robbery. He thought the ring to be thousands of years old with ancient Greek writing on it."

"Maybe you're right, Danny, but I need to get back to my customers. Enjoy your stay, Miss."

"Thank you. I shall."

Danny escorted Violet back to their table as a barmaid brought food from the kitchen.

"What is this?' Violet asked.

"Shepherd's pie. Now here's a dish guaranteed to put some meat on your bones."

"Danny, I can't let you pay for this."

"Don't insult me, girlie. Lady Alice has paid all my back wages, and if I want to spend some of my money on a pretty American, who's to stop me?"

Violet smiled. "It's very gracious of you. I accept your kind invitation to lunch." She inhaled deeply. "It smells wonderful."

"Go on. Dig in."

Violet broke through the bread crust with a spoon and took a bite. "By golly. This is delicious. It's layers of meat with potatoes and vegetables."

"Haven't you had Shepherd's pie before?"

"We cook something similar in the States, but we call it a pot pie, usually using chicken." Violet dove in with relish. She hadn't recovered from the skimpy meals served to the servants at Bosworth. Even with the food provided by Miss Mona, the portions doled out by the cook were still parsimonious, but this pie would go a long way making up for it. "Danny, you mentioned there were symbols on the ring. How would you know? Did Lady Alice show you the ring?"

"Her Great Dane swallowed it once."

Violet made a face.

"I was asked to retrieve the ring and clean it for Her Ladyship."

"Unpleasant."

Danny chortled, "Not really. I got out of work while following the dog for two days until things worked themselves out."

"Wouldn't it have been better to pin the dog up until the ring appeared again?"

"I would think so, but Lady Alice wouldn't have stood for it. She really loved that big galoot of a dog."

"I guess you don't remember the symbols on the ring."

Danny puffed up his chest. "I made a copy of the symbols. It was such an unusual ring, it made me curious. I thought the local reverend would be able to translate the Latin inscription, but he said it was Greek and couldn't translate it for me."

Violet tried to hide her excitement. "You were so smart to think of such a thing. After we get back, may I see the copy?"

"Sure," Danny said happily, thinking he was impressing Violet. Perhaps if he could prove himself a valuable asset to Violet, he might be lucky enough to be given a kiss. Danny was not immune to the idea of a little romance.

Violet looked at her watch. "Danny, we best be going. The cobbler said the shoe repairs would be finished by now."

"Right you are, Violet. Let's be off." Danny threw coins on the table and waved goodbye to Jansen who looked curiously after them.

"The American is after something. I hope she doesn't hurt Danny in her search," Jansen remarked to the barmaid.

"Danny's a big boy. He can take care of himself. She's but a wee thing."

Jansen muttered, "That's not the kind of hurt I'm talking about. She might break his heart."

The barmaid sneered. "Will serve Danny right after all the hearts he's broken amongst the local birdies."

"He was just a young bloke having a bit of fun."

"Is that what you men call hurting the feelings of young girls? A bit of fun? Instead of breaking Danny's heart, I hope the American tears it out."

"You're a bitter one," Jansen said.

"You should talk with all your chatter about gettin' revenge on Bosworth Manor and Lady Alice. There has been rumors about goings-on at Bosworth. You have anything to do with it?"

"Get on with your work, lass, and keep your mouth shut if you know what's good for you."

The barmaid shot Jansen a look of disgust before waiting on a customer.

Jansen walked over to the window and observed Danny and Violet enter the cobbler's shop. Next time Danny came into the pub, he would have a little chat with him. Beware of Americans asking questions.

18

Mona, Farley, and Alice met in the priest hole after dinner.

"Alice and I searched the tunnels and secret corridors. The gate guarding the main tunnel is locked up tight. No sign of entry."

"Then I would say the break-in was an inside job," Mona concurred.

"I'm not so sure," Alice said. "I've been searching for the original plans of Bosworth Manor. Through the years, knowledge of all the original tunnels and corridors has been lost. There may be more of which we are not aware."

"It must be an inside job," Mona repeated.

"Then it would have to be either George or Danny. I can't see those maids having either the gumption or the intelligence," Alice said.

Mona suggested, "Their families could be under threat, and the girls are simply carrying out orders."

"I told you they were poor girls from the village. They have no one. I took them in as an act of charity."

"They could be a plant," Farley said.

Alice clicked her tongue. "I've known these lasses all their lives. They lost their families through misfortune. If they are some criminal masterminds, then I'm the queen of England."

Mona acquiesced. "Let's move on. Violet brought us some good news. Apparently your Great Dane swallowed your amethyst ring, and you had Danny retrieve it."

"That's correct."

"Danny was interested in the markings on the ring and wrote down the symbols. He gave Violet a copy."

"What's my ring have to do with anything?"

"From your own description, it was the only thing of value stolen that night."

"Let me see these markings," Farley demanded.

Mona handed him the copy. "Farley, do you

remember where you bought the ring?"

"I bought it in Venice for Alice. I was told it was made in the sixteen hundreds. The amethyst was a startling color and of great clarity. It was like nothing I had ever seen before, and I knew it had been crafted by a master."

"It was very heavy," Alice remarked.

"It was a large ring," Farley added.

"Were there other stones on it?"

"No, just a huge amethyst stone surrounded by gold."

"Where was the lettering on the ring?"

"Around the stone," Lady Alice answered.

"Was there anything else stamped or carved into the ring?"

Farley pointed to letters on the copy. "These letters were on the inside of the ring."

"Did you have a jeweler look at it?"

Lady Alice hesitated for a few seconds, glancing at Farley. "The ring was a gift, so I never had it appraised."

Farley stated, "Mona, you're good with languages. Don't you agree they look like Greek letters?"

"It does, but I'm not sure how old they are

though. The Greek alphabet went through various stages of development."

"There is a professor of languages at Balliol College in Oxford. He is a friend of mine. Why don't I give him a ring, and we have him translate these letters?" Farley offered.

Mona said, "I think it is a splendid idea."

"Good. I'll make the appointment for tomorrow morning. We should all go and make the day of it."

"Sounds like a plan, and I look forward to it. I'm sorry Robert and Mona, but I'm off to bed. Exploring those corridors has turned my legs into jelly."

"I'll escort you to your room, Alice. I don't like the thought of the two of you roaming this house after dark until we know what is going on."

"Mona, are you coming?" Alice asked.

"Yes, indeed, but I'll probably be up late reading your father's journal. He made some unusual notes in it, and I'd like to read through them again."

Farley asked, "Do you have a notion?"

"I am starting to form a theory but it is so fantastic, I am loath to share it."

"Oh, please do."

"No, I'll wait until after we see the professor. Until then, my lips are sealed."

"Party pooper," Farley said.

Mona followed Farley and Alice up the stairs. She knew Farley was bursting with curiosity about her theory, but she had no proof. Her theory was so implausible, she could hardly fathom it herself, but if she was right, history would be turned on its ear. It was one of the few times in Mona's life she hoped she was wrong.

19

Farley shook hands with Professor Nithercott as he introduced his party. "Nithercott, thank you for allowing us to come on such short notice. May I introduce Lady Alice Morrell and Miss Mona Moon."

Lady Alice clasped his hand as well. "You have no idea how much this means, Professor Nithercott."

"Please call me Ogden or Nithercott if you feel the need for distance." Nithercott beckoned them to sit as he retreated behind a massive desk littered with various papers and charts. "Your call intrigued me, Robert. You say you may have a ring thousands of years old with Greek letters. Now of course, many rings have been discovered with Greek writing, both ancient and current.

Usually it's the name of the owner or a seal used for important documents or letters."

Farley said, "We may be wasting your time, Nithercott, but we have to know and you're the man for the job."

"Bring it on then."

Mona handed him a copy of the ring's inscription.

"Is this the correct order of the letters?"

"It's a copy of a copy. I wrote it exactly as it was given to me."

"Hmm. Very well, then." Ogden Nithercott put the writing under a magnifying glass and turned it this way and that way. He stared at it for a long time before clearing his throat. "Robert, you say you bought this ring in Venice."

"The antique dealer said it was old but not ancient."

"What did the ring look like?"

Lady Alice pulled a small photograph from her purse and handed it to Nithercott. "This picture was taken for insurance purposes."

"And the center stone was an amethyst?"

Lady Alice replied, "Yes."

Professor Nithercott examined the photograph closely. "Amethysts were purported to have mystical properties of healing and piety. The Bible mentions the amethyst as one of the twelve stones to be worn on the breastplate of the high priest. The ancient Greeks believed amethysts protected one from drunkenness. If one drank wine from a goblet made entirely from an amethyst, they could not get drunk. The gemstone is still used to adorn crosses of our Christian clergy."

He leaned forward toward Mona. "What are these letters here?"

"I was told they were on the inside of the ring."

Tapping his fingers on the desk, Dr. Nithercott studied the copy intently before copying the letters in a notebook. "I think you really got something here."

"What do you mean?" Farley inquired.

Turning the copy of the letters around to them, Nithercott used a pencil as a pointer. "See these letters? This is ancient Greek meaning *Son of Zeus.*"

"Yes, I see," Lady Alice said.

"These letters here—Ἀλέξανδρος," he said,

pointing, "refer to a name."

"What name, Professor?" Alice asked.

"The ring says Aléxandros, Son of Zeus."

Excited, Mona stood, saying, "We know Aléxandros as Alexander, and there was only one Alexander who was declared a son of Zeus."

Lady Alice gasped, "And we call him Alexander the Great!"

20

"**Y**ou're off your chump, Nithercott. Obviously, I was sold a tourist piece," Farley blurted out.

Nithercott looked at the photograph again. "I can't tell you how many inscriptions I have translated from Alexander's timeline, and the ring in this photograph looks spot on as the real item. Also the letters are correct. The writing is where most forgers make their mistake. They either use an alphabet system from the wrong era or refer to him as Alexander the Great. He was not called *great* until after his death in 323 BC. During his lifetime, Alexander would have been referred to as Alexander III, King of Macedon, King of Persia, or Lord of Asia. His most prized title would have been Son of Zeus as it would have conferred the title of a god upon him."

Alice asked, "Why did Alexander think he was the offspring of Zeus?"

"His mother, Olympias, claimed her womb was struck by a thunderbolt on the night of her marriage to Philip II. The thunderbolt was the weapon wielded by Zeus, the king of all the Greek gods."

"Maybe Philip was just damn good in bed, thus the pyrotechnics," Farley said, taking out his cigarette case.

"Robert, don't be gauche," Alice admonished.

Nithercott frowned and said, "Farley, would you not? Be a good chap. I don't let anyone smoke in here. Even myself."

"Sorry," Farley muttered, putting his cigarette case away.

Nithercott continued with his narration. "Olympias was the first person to claim Alexander was the son of Zeus. The second authority was the oracle at the Oasis of Amun Ra in ancient Libya who also made the same claim when Alexander came calling. Of course, what else was the oracle to do with Alexander's army standing outside his door? The oasis is now located inside Egyptian borders and called Siwa."

"Do you really think Alexander believed he was the son of Zeus?" Mona asked.

The professor thought for a moment before speaking. "I think he did. Zeus and his pantheon of gods were just as real to Alexander as our God is to us today. Are you a follower of Jesus, Miss Moon?"

"I try to be."

"And do you believe with all your heart?"

"I have doubts at times."

"As do most people, but you worship and claim to be a Christian. It was probably the same for Alexander. He believed in Zeus, worshipped according to the customs of the day, but may have had doubts in the back of his mind depending on whether he had a good breakfast or not."

Farley chuckled. "I didn't know the status of religious belief was based on the digestion of one's meals."

"Even Jesus knew the importance of feeding the flock before preaching. The story of the two fishes and five loaves of bread. Loads of symbolism there."

Alice said, "Let's get back to Alexander."

Nithercott smiled showing off his perfectly straight teeth—an unusual trait in an Englishman, but he was typically English in every other way. He possessed patrician features, brown hair slicked back by pomade, wore a custom tailored tweed suit with the outline of a pipe and tobacco bin in his coat pocket. He was not handsome like Farley. Nithercott's face resembled that of a Bassett hound, all droopy except for his eyes, which were lively and alert. It was Nithercott's confidence and boldness which made him attractive. No doubt he had his share of admirers among the fairer sex.

"I have a friend at the British Museum who specializes in alloys used for jewelry in the ancient world. Let me ring him. At the very least, he will be able to determine if the ring was made in the time of Alexander."

"Do you think the ring could be authentic?" Mona asked, watching Nithercott closely.

"The ring is curious as it does not have the image of Alexander on it. Rings, medallions, and coins certainly would have the image of Alexander to honor him. It was the public relations of the day. We pretty much have a good idea of what Alexander looked like. He had blond or light brown hair and exhibited heterochromia iridum, which was another sign of being a god."

Farley asked, "What's heterochromia iridum?

"It's a highfaluting term meaning Alexander had one blue eye and one brown eye," Mona said.

"Why didn't you just say so, Nithercott?" Farley complained.

"Because I wanted to sound incredibly erudite when I am in the company of two such beautiful women." Nithercott stared at Mona and mumbled, "And such rare lovelies." He jumped up and raced around the desk to stand in front of Mona. "My dear, are your eyes yellow?"

"I refer to them as amber."

"The effect is startling, even more so with your platinum hair. Your coloring is the result of thousands and thousands of years of breeding resulting in rare recessive genes. Perhaps only a thousand people in the world have eyes such as yours. I have a geneticist friend who would love to obtain a sample of your blood and perhaps a small skin biopsy."

"These traits run in my family."

"You mean there are more like you?"

"Let's stay on track," Farley said.

Nithercott turned his attention to Alice, taking her hand gently in his. "And you, my dear, are the crowning glory of British propagation with your black hair and blue eyes—a perfect English rose."

"Oh, my goodness," Alice sputtered, pulling back her hand.

"Professor Nithercott, I've read about the new field of genetics, but can we stay on point?" Mona asked.

"Perhaps both you ladies would like to join me for luncheon. I can regale you with stories of both ancient and cutting-edge technology now being studied at Oxford."

"Alexander," Mona reminded Nithercott.

"Yes, but he's dead and I'm very much alive."

"Professor Nithercott, let me remind you that we traveled several hours to get here. Now please focus," Mona chided.

Nithercott sighed and returned to his chair, looking despondent. "Farley, why did you bring such glorious angels within my sphere only to cruelly deprive me of their company so quickly? It's not fair that you alone should benefit from their companionship."

Ignoring Nithercott's banter, Alice asked, "What do these letters mean? They were on the inside of the ring."

"Roxanne."

"The Bactrian wife of Alexander. That Roxanne?" Alice inquired.

"The only female other than his mother whom Alexander was purported to love. He fell in love with Roxanne at first sight, just like I'm doing now," Nithercott said as he sidled up to Alice.

Mona said, "You say the ring is curious because it doesn't have the image of Alexander on it."

"Let's say the ring was made during Alexander's time," Nithercott mused. "If it was made for his compatriots or for anyone who was an admirer of Alexander, they would have had Alexander's image put on the ring. The fact that the ring has an amethyst gives it special meaning because of the magical importance attributed to the stone. It could be a personal ring made for Alexander to wear."

"What are you saying, Professor Nithercott?" Mona asked.

"Fantastic," Farley mutter. "Simply fantastic."

"My ring might have been worn by Alexander himself?" Alice asked. Not waiting for Nithercott to answer, she asked, "Mona, what do you think?"

"I think Professor Nithercott might be on to something, Alice, but not in the way you think. I have been over your father's journal several times now, and he speaks of finding an important piece of jewelry at the archeological site with the letters AG beside the notation. On his last entry, he states he knows the attack is imminent and believes he will die. He wrote that he hid AG's ring where it will never be found. The last entry implied Colonel Morrell believed the attack was planned to recover the ring, and he didn't want it to fall into al-Sharif's hands."

"And you think AG stands for Alexander the Great?" Alice asked.

"What's that got to do with the ring I bought for Alice? I bought Alice's ring in Venice years before Colonel Morrell and Alice went to Mesopotamia. There can't be a connection."

Mona disagreed vehemently. "Let's say Colonel Morrell did stumble upon a ring thought to be worn by Alexander. Maybe the signet ring he gave to Perdiccas, his bodyguard. Professor, would people kill over such a discovery?"

"Indeed they would, Miss Moon. To find the signet ring of Alexander would have political significance even today, especially in the Far East where things are so volatile. With the signet ring which substitutes for a crown and scepter, anyone could declare a divine line from Alexander until present day. Alexander the Great is still revered in the Far East and India. It would give the owner of the ring political and spiritual cache."

"But Alexander gave his signet ring to Perdiccas, his bodyguard, on his deathbed in Babylon," Mona recounted.

"Near where Father was stationed."

Nithercott said, "The question remains as to what Perdiccas did with the ring. He did not claim to be Alexander's heir, but instead threw his support to Alexander's wife, Roxanne, and her unborn child. Perhaps he passed the ring to her. It was a symbol of great importance to help her child succeed in his father's place. There is another notation from history about Alexander's ring. John of Antioch give an account that the Roman Emperor Caracalla removed Alexander's ring from his tomb."

"In Greece?" Farley asked.

"Alexander's body was stolen by Ptolemy and taken to Egypt."

"Where is he now?"

"Farley, your guess is as good as mine. There are expeditions now trying to find Alexander's tomb in Alexandria. Others say his body was taken to Venice by Christians under the guise of being Saint Mark's body, the patron saint of Venice, and now lies under the altar in St. Mark's Basilica."

"The connection with Venice again," Farley said. "This story has so many twists and turns it is like a maze."

"Is John of Antioch writing about Alexander's official signet ring or a personal ring given to him by Roxanne?" Mona mused.

Farley added, "Or even by his good buddy, Hephaestion."

Mona shifted in her chair. "Let's not muddy the waters with Hephaestion."

"If I can show my friend the ring, he can

throw some light on your story. At the very least, he can tell you if the ring is a fake," Nithercott offered.

"That will be difficult," Alice said. "The ring was stolen about a month ago."

"Oh, a downside to be sure. How bloody awful, but still my friend might be able to tell something from the photograph."

"Even with one so small?" Alice inquired.

"He might. Let's give it a go, my beautiful English rose."

Farley declared, "I'm lost. Are we discussing my ring to Alice or the ring found in Mesopotamia?"

"Alice's ring. We don't have enough information at the moment about Colonel Morrell's ring. All we do know is that a ring of great importance may be involved, may have a personal connection with Alexander, and someone may think Alice's ring is connected with the ring in her father's journal," Mona said.

"Why don't we have the police check the pawn shops?" Nithercott recommended.

Farley chuckled and said, "Do you think the thief would have taken such a ring to the local pawn shop for a few quid? I tell you the ring is in a safe, probably in a Swiss deposit box by now."

Mona asked, "Could your father have switched rings without your knowledge, Alice?"

"He never wrote to me of such a discovery, and after you and I left Iraq, I never saw Father alive again. He wouldn't have had the opportunity."

"What about his possessions sent back with his body?"

"I've gone through them. There were no rings except for his wedding ring which he still wore and an ancestral ring bearing our family's crest."

"How do you know? You said you never saw his body when it came home."

"I had George take the rings from his hands. It's a wonder they weren't stolen in Iraq."

"Ah, so someone did view the body," Mona murmured. "Where are they now?"

"In my jewelry box."

"Were they in the jewelry box the night of the robbery?"

"Yes."

"Is your family's signet ring worth a significant amount?"

"Some. It has a band made from rubies."

"Yet a gold wedding band and another ring with rubies were not taken."

After looking at his watch, Nithercott clapped his hands. "Golly, the time has flown by, so let's take the next logical step. My friend is probably home for lunch. Let's pop over and see him. He would know much more about ancient jewelry than I."

"I have a car outside," Farley offered. "I hope you don't think I was going to stay in this stuffy office while you traipse off on a grand adventure with these sirens."

"It can take all of us," Alice said.

Nithercott jumped up and raced for his hat. Opening the door, he beckoned, "Goddesses first."

"It's about time some man recognized what I was," Mona said, stepping into the hallway.

They hurried to the parked car.

Farley took the lead and started the car while the others piled in. Mona sat beside Farley while Alice took the back seat with Nithercott.

Nithercott pointed out items of interest to Lady Alice as they drove out of town, trying to engage her in small talk.

They were heading for a stone bridge when Mona screamed, "FARLEY! LOOK OUT!"

A lorry veered into their lane and broadsided them. A dark sedan driving behind the lorry pulled up alongside Farley's car. Two men jumped out and violently pulled Alice, kicking and screaming, from the Duesenberg. Nithercott fought off a third man pummeling him through a broken window. Once Alice was secure in the other car, it sped off, leaving behind an unconscious Farley, a dazed and bleeding Mona, and an injured Nithercott.

Mona stumbled out of the car trying to get the license plate number of the speeding car but fell to the ground. She lay on the road in shock.

Alice had been kidnapped!

21

"Where am I?" Farley asked, trying to get his bearings.

"You're at the John Radcliffe Hospital in Headington, Farley."

"What happened?"

Mona helped Farley to sit up. "We were hit by a truck, and Alice was kidnapped. Nithercott is pretty beat up, but the hospital has released him. He's waiting outside."

Holding his head in his hands, Farley said, "Oh, is that all?"

Mona called out into the hallway. "Nurse, His Lordship is conscious. Can you call the doctor?"

"I don't need a doctor," Farley insisted, pushing out of bed. "I need my trousers."

"Please sit down before you fall. You're in no

condition to be leaving."

"Where are my trousers, I say?"

"The nurse had to cut them off. There was so much blood she thought your legs were injured. The staff didn't have time to take your pants off gently and neatly fold them the way your valet would. I have all your possessions though—your wallet and such."

"You can drive. We have to go after Alice."

"There is no car to drive, Farley. It's been totaled."

Farley groaned.

"I hope you had it insured."

"What about Alice?"

"The police are doing a door by door search. She won't get far," Mona said, trying to reassure Farley.

"I can't fail Alice again. Not again."

"How have you failed Alice?"

Farley was in a panic searching for his clothes. "I was beastly to her when I came back from the War. She tried to help me, but I wouldn't let her. I drove her away."

"You were suffering from shellshock."

"Is that the name for it? I call it being a bastard."

"Did it ever occur to you that perhaps you had fallen out of love with Alice and didn't want to marry her?"

"NO!"

"Maybe she didn't want to marry you either. Since both of you are typically English, neither one of you told the other the truth about your feelings."

"I made a promise to marry her."

"Exactly. She made a promise to marry you when both of you were only eighteen years old. You were still babies. 'Tis a shame that perhaps you grew up wanting different things from Alice."

"You don't know what you're talking about. Where are my clothes?" Farley bolted about the room, nearly losing his hospital gown.

"NURSE! HURRY! Your patient is about to flee with his derriere exposed for the world to see."

Mona sauntered out of the room as several nurses rushed in. It was her guess they would put Farley in a public ward now to keep a closer watch on him. He was being most difficult. As she made her way to the reception hall, Mona wondered if Farley would later recall that he had given a clear view of his nether regions.

She hadn't minded. Not at all. It had been the only bright spot of the day.

22

Mona hired another car after agents from Scotland Yard arrived at the hospital and questioned the three of them. Farley raved about Alexander the Great while she and Nithercott shrugged and swore they didn't know what Farley was talking about. Must be the bump on the head they told the inspectors.

Afterward, Mona drove to Bosworth Manor with Nithercott moaning in the front seat of a Ford sedan and Farley groaning in the back.

Violet rushed out as Mona stopped the car near the front door. "Oh, Miss!"

"It looks worse than it is, Violet."

"But the stitches on your face!"

"They will leave a scar to be sure, but my disfigurement will provide fodder at future cocktail parties."

Danny helped Nithercott out of the car and shot an uncertain look at Mona.

"I'll explain the bumps and bruises later. Get Professor Nithercott into a bedroom next to Farley. Violet will get me settled."

"Yes, Miss. What else is needed?"

"George, have someone stay with Farley all night. Can you contact the village doctor?"

"I'll call immediately."

"Good. See how soon he can arrive. Has there been any communication about Lady Alice?"

"No, Miss. Not a peep. No telegrams. No calls except from the police. No letters."

"Are there local men you can trust, George?"

"Yes. Quite a few."

"Call them, and have them stand guard. I think contact will be made tonight, but I'm too tired to stand watch myself. Farley and Nithercott are certainly in no shape to do so."

"This is a dreadful turn of events."

Mona patted George's shoulder. "We'll get Lady Alice back, safe and sound."

"All I can think of is the Lindbergh baby kidnapping. That didn't turn out so happily," George said, referring to the 1932 murder of Charles and

Anne Lindbergh's twenty-month-old son, who was kidnapped from his nursery and murdered.

"Don't think of it, George. We'll get her back. Lady Alice is no dummy, and she'll do what is necessary in order to stay alive."

Violet put her arm around Mona's waist. "Miss, your bandages are bleeding. Let's get you cleaned up properly and put to bed."

"I need something to eat, Violet."

"I'll take care of it, Miss. How about two nice soft boiled eggs and toast with peach marmalade? Maybe a cup of broth? You should eat food that won't be too hard on your stomach."

"Can you see about trays for the gents?"

"I'll take them a tray after you are in bed, and I'll stay with Lord Farley until the doctor arrives. Come now. I'll help you up the stairs."

As Violet led Mona up the staircase, Mona looked down at the scurrying servants and advised, "George, if I were you, I'd get out those hunting shotguns and load them. Who knows what the night will bring?"

"I was in the Boer War with Colonel Morrell in 1899, Miss. I know how to handle myself in a crisis. Just give me a moment to adjust, and I'll be right as rain."

"Good man," Mona mumbled as Violet led her upstairs. "Good man."

23

Mona awoke to discover Farley standing over her with a startled expression.

"Egad, you look awful."

"My head had a run-in with your dashboard. If you think I look bad, you should see Nithercott's pulverized face."

"I have. He's uglier than ever."

"That's not a nice thing to say about your friend."

"I don't feel very nice this morning."

"Shouldn't you be recovering in bed?"

"That's a lovely invitation." Farley climbed into Mona's bed and fluffed a pillow before burrowing under the covers.

"I meant in your own bed."

"Don't be an old stick. I feel faint."

"You're a fraud. I think I shall ring for Danny and have you taken back to your own domicile."

"Seriously, Mona. I need to talk with you. I don't remember much of what happened."

"What do you remember?"

"I remember hearing screaming and the impact of the truck as it hit us. Nothing afterwards. A total blank."

Mona explained, "Another car flanked us. Three men jumped out. Two grabbed Alice and another broke a window to beat Nithercott who was trying to save her. I was dazed, and you were knocked unconscious. It was fast and efficient. Obviously a professional hit. Any news about Alice?"

"The police were here earlier. Nothing yet."

"What time is it?"

"A little after eight in the morning."

"If you had the strength to go downstairs, you can go back to your room on your own power."

Farley slid deeper under the covers. "I do feel light-headed, so I think I should stay put. Besides, there's nothing to do until we hear from Alice's captors. So sleep, my Sleeping Beauty. We'll be no good for Alice if we drop dead on our feet."

"We'll do her no good wallowing between her

sheets all day either."

"Shut up and move over. You're taking up too much room," Farley complained.

"What!"

"I'm exhausted. You're exhausted. Violet's exhausted. George is beyond exhausted. He was up all night standing guard, so I have sent the staff to bed. The entire house is shut down until everyone recovers from sleep deprivation. Now move over. I'm totally knackered and too sore to walk back to my room. I just had to make sure you were all right."

"Someone has to stay awake in case the captors send a telegram or phone with their demands."

"I sent for my father's security men to handle the police or any calls. They are currently downstairs. Now shush, woman. I have a monster of a headache." Farley pushed Mona over and turned on his side, determined to stay.

Mona knew it was going to cause a scandal, but she let him settle in and fall asleep. There was something calming about his measured breathing.

She hunkered down in the bed, wondering about the fate of the dark beauty Alice, and drifted off to a dreamless slumber.

24

Noisy footsteps in the hallway stirred Mona. She groggily looked at her travel clock. It said seven p.m. Stiff and sore, Mona struggled into the bathroom and took a shower, inspecting her body. It was no surprise to her that bruises covered her arms and chest, not to mention her battered mug, although she was sure the swelling would calm down in a day or two. She changed the bandages on the side of her face and neck. The stitches in her face itched, but she dared not scratch them.

Resigned to pain, Mona struggled to put on a pair of slacks and a loose blouse. Where was Violet when she needed her? A jolt shot through Mona.

Where was Violet?

Mona rushed to Violet's room and peeked inside without knocking. Violet's purse was on a chest and her pajamas were laid out on the bed. Mona looked in the cupboard. Violet's trunk was still there. But where was she?

Mona grabbed her gun and crept down the dark staircase. Somewhere a door slammed. Mona jumped, then hunkered down and peered through the banister.

Two strange men guarded the front entrance, ignoring George who carried an empty bottle of scotch on a silver tray from the library.

Hmm, an empty liquor bottle. Farley must be up and about.

Sighing with relief, Mona continued down the staircase.

Noticing a gun in her hand, the two men jumped up and trained their guns on her.

"Boys, I'm just passing through. No need to get excited."

"State your name and purpose," one of the men ordered, challenging Mona.

Nithercott stumbled through the library door and found himself the target of a cocked pistol. He threw his hands up.

"Nithercott, what are you up to?" Farley asked, peering around the library door. He quickly took in the scene. "Boys, you know the Professor. Nithercott, put your hands down. They won't shoot you."

"What about the woman?" one of the men asked.

Farley glanced around Nithercott. "Mona! You have finally risen from the dead and in time for dinner, too." He winked at his men. "Don't worry, men. This is Mona Moon, and she always carries a gun, although it has done no good keeping her from danger. I'm not even sure the gun has bullets."

Farley's cavalier response galled Mona. She turned and fired a round into the wainscot. "I assure you my gun has bullets."

"Golly, Mona! You've marred the wainscoting."

Nithercott said, "Please excuse me for a moment. I feel a need to change my pants." He bounded around Mona and up the stairs.

"Farley, are you drunk?"

Farley replied, "No, I am not, but I have taken a pain draught, courtesy of the local doctor, and it seems to be working quite nicely. I feel no pain. In fact, I feel nothing. Here, pull on my lip. Go on pull on it. I shan't feel a thing."

Mona pushed by Farley into the library.

He followed, staggering slightly.

Mona looked at the used glasses on the various tables in the library. "You have been drinking. How are we going to help Alice if you are drunk?"

"Speaking of Alice."

"Yes?"

"Nothing."

"Nothing?"

Farley shook his head.

Mona laid her gun on the mantel. "Have the police been in touch?"

"They came this afternoon. The house-to-house search was fruitless. There was no trace of Alice. Tomorrow morning they start beating the bushes."

"So they have given up on a rescue and are in a recovery mode?"

"We must be prepared for the worst."

"I won't give up. They wouldn't have taken Alice just to kill her."

"Mona, there hasn't been any contact. No ransom demands."

"Then why was Alice taken?"

"I can think of several horrible reasons."

"The abduction was a professional job. Orchestrated. I'm sure it has to do with the threatening letters."

"It might have to do with revenge for something her father did in Mesopotamia."

"The men were English. I heard them speak."

"What were their accents?"

"Cockney. If Alice was taken for revenge, Englishmen would not have been hired. Men from the Near East would do their own killing. It's a point of honor with them."

Before Farley could answer, Nithercott entered the room. "Did they break your nose, too, Mona?"

Mona gave a tired smile. "No, my head bounced off the dashboard, cutting my face."

"That explains the bandages and the swelling around your eyes. Still, you look smashing."

"Very kind of you to say so, Professor."

"Am I interrupting a private conversation?"

"Farley and I were discussing where to go

from here. Any ideas?"

"I think the guards should be sent away as well as the staff."

"I agree with Nithercott," Mona said. "I think Alice's abductors will make contact when they think it is safe. Every moment that contact is delayed, Alice is in a more desperate situation."

"My brain may be fuzzy, but why would the kidnappers contact us? We can't give them any money because Alice doesn't have any."

"Perhaps they think we will raise money on her behalf," Nithercott suggested.

"How?" Farley said. "Both Mona and I have holdings in America. It would take time to wire money from Kentucky."

"But you both are rich, and you were engaged to Alice," Nithercott argued.

"What I want to know is how the kidnappers knew we were leaving your office, Professor?" Mona asked.

"It didn't come from me, if that's what you are accusing, dear lady. I knew Farley was coming, but had no idea that Lady Alice or you would join him. The perpetrators knew because they were watching."

"Hmm."

"You don't seem convinced, Miss Moon. I didn't get this battered face because I was conniving with the enemy. I got beaten up because I was trying to save Lady Alice. Look at us. We are a sorry lot. You look like someone took a cricket bat to you. Farley had to be hospitalized and is now on pain medication, which he may well become addicted to again."

Mona jerked her head up at Nithercott's last statement. The reason for Alice's estrangement with Farley was now cleared. Everything made sense. It's why they didn't marry when Farley came home in early 1919. Farley had become addicted to pain medication during the war and spent years trying to break free. Alice spent her youth trying to help Farley kick the habit until she could stand no more, calling off their engagement. Alice's wasted youth is the debt Farley feels he can never repay.

She felt deep sorrow at her friends' lost innocence and stolen happiness because a crazed Yugoslav nationalist assassinated Archduke Franz Ferdinand, heir to the Austro-Hungarian Empire. The murder caused the Great War and swept up

Farley, Alice, and her brother into its great maul with 19 million deaths and the collapse of the Ottoman Empire and the ruling houses of Germany and Russia.

If that wasn't devastating enough, the Spanish Flu rode on the heels of the Great War infecting over 500 million people world-wide and causing the deaths of 50 million plus, an estimated three percent of the world's population. It was a wonder Alice and Farley had survived.

Farley and Alice had suffered enough. Alice shouldn't be asked to endure retribution for her father's sins or the sins of the world for that matter.

"Again I ask, where do we go from here?" Mona asked, feeling inadequate to the task of finding Lady Alice. She was grasping at straws. "I feel we haven't been contacted because the kidnappers don't think it's safe to do so."

"I agree with you, Mona," Nithercott said. "Let's send the servants to safety in the village and dismiss Farley's men."

"Don't I have anything to say about this?" Farley snapped.

"No, you're drunk and out of your mind with

fear for Alice," Mona replied, grabbing the drink out of Farley's hand and throwing its contents into the fireplace.

"Blimey, Mona!" Farley exclaimed, looking at her in surprise.

"Nithercott, take His Lordship upstairs for a cold shower and throw away his pain medication. Farley will just have to punch through any discomfort."

Moving toward Farley, Nithercott grinned and said "Gladly, Mona."

Farley ran from him, but Nithercott grabbed the collar of his jacket and the seat of his pants. "Now don't be a wanker, Farley. Mona's right. You're no good to anyone smashed like this."

"Nithercott, have you seen Violet?"

"She's in the kitchen helping to prepare food."

"I'll instruct the staff to leave. You take care of your charge."

"What about his guard dogs?"

"Farley, tell your men to leave."

"No!"

Mona lied, "I am the executor of Alice's estate and her in absence, I make the rules. If you don't order them to vacate, I will force you out of the house. Nithercott and I will try to save Alice on our own, and once again, you will have failed her."

Farley pleaded with Mona. "Don't, Mona. Please don't."

"Then go with Nithercott and don't give us any more trouble."

"Please let go, old chap. Let me have some dignity. I'll tell the men to leave."

Nithercott relinquished and said to Mona, "Righto, see you in a bit. Come on, Farley, we're going upstairs."

Mona waited in the library while Farley told his men to leave and heard the front door open and close. She sat in a chair, and upon giving the two men time to reach the upstairs, Mona went in search of Violet.

25

"I won't do it. You need my help," Violet insisted as Mona threw Violet's clothes into an overnight bag.

"Take only what you need. I've called the village inn and they have reserved rooms for the staff, including you."

Violet snatched clothes from the suitcase and threw them on the floor. "I won't desert you. Look at you. You're all banged up. Who will change your bandage? Who will help you dress?"

Mona grabbed Violet by the shoulders. "Violet, you must go. I'm counting on you to take charge of Lady Alice's staff. Everything has been worked out with the innkeeper. You and the others should leave as soon as possible. Please, you must be an adult about this."

Violet burst into tears. "For how long, Miss?"

"As long as it takes. Here's a hanky. Why do you never have a hanky on you, Violet?"

"Because I love the smell of yours, Miss" Violet replied, sniffling.

"I will buy you a bottle of perfume after this is over. Something light and fresh to remind you of spring. All young girls should smell like spring, don't you think?"

Violet blew her nose. "If you say so, Miss."

Mona repacked Violet's clothes. "That should be enough to get you through a couple of days. Now remember, put all food on the room tab, but remind the staff I won't pay for liquor. That's on them."

Mona picked up the suitcase and herded Violet down the stairs, saying, "And everyone is to stay near the inn. We might we need them. Everyone means Danny and George. The maids can go home if they wish."

"This is their home."

"Oh, yes, I forgot. Then they must stay at the inn for now."

Mona and Violet stopped on the landing.

The staff was waiting by the front door and

looked up expectantly at them.

"What about your meals?" Violet asked, ready to break into tears again.

Mona whispered, "I know this is hard for you to believe but I took care of myself for many years before I met you. Now put on a brave face in front of the others. The cars are waiting."

Violet followed Mona down the staircase, stopping before the little knot of confused employees.

"George, you have your instructions."

"That I do, Miss, but permit me to say I feel this is foolish."

"Permission denied." Mona pushed through the front doors and opened the doors of two idling cars. "They will take you into town. Stay there until you hear from me again."

George and Danny reluctantly loaded everyone's luggage and helped the girls into the front car. They got into the second one.

Mona patted the hood of the front car and went quickly inside so she did not have to see Violet's fearful face pressed against the car window. She breathed a little easier. Even though she was eleven years older than Violet, Mona felt as protective of her as a mother would a child.

Now that the staff had gone, Mona could really investigate Alice's disappearance. She bounded up the stairs to her room to find a sweater as it was chilly. Then she intended to help Nithercott with Farley.

Mona opened the door to her room and screamed.

A message was scrawled on the mirror of the vanity in Mona's Passion Pink lipstick.

Give us what we want or Lady Alice dies!

26

"You were right, Mona," Nithercott said, handing her a stiff Irish whisky. "The kidnappers contacted us as soon as they saw the cars leave."

Mona pushed the drink away. "No, thank you. I want my head to be clear."

"Whoever they are, they have access to the house," Farley said.

Nithercott concurred. "And have had all along. That's how they knew you were coming to my office."

Mona stood and called out, "WE DON'T KNOW WHAT YOU WANT! TELL US AND WE'LL GET IT! WE JUST WANT LADY ALICE BACK SAFE!"

Farley, Mona, and Nithercott were silent for a long time until Nithercott said, "We need to push on."

"There must be more hidden corridors in this mausoleum than Alice knew. She's got to be here somewhere," Farley said, his voice filled with anger. "I'll tear this place apart brick by brick if I have to."

"I'm sure Alice won't appreciate you demolishing her home," Mona said. "Let's get some food into you, Farley, and then we'll begin the great hunt."

"How do you know the food hasn't been poisoned by our *friends*?" Nithercott asked.

Farley complained, "This keeps getting worse and worse."

"Because they need us to find something for them. They'll only try to murder us after they get what they want. At the moment, we're too valuable."

"Do you know what *it* is?" Nithercott said, following Mona to the kitchen.

"I have a vague theory."

"What is it?"

Mona threw a loaf of bread at Farley, who began slicing with a bread knife. Nithercott rummaged through the refrigerator and found cold cuts and mustard. They quickly made some sandwiches.

"Not here," Mona said, leading them out to some chairs under an old yew tree. "Let's turn the chairs toward the tree. No doubt someone is peering at us with a pair of binoculars from one of the windows. I don't want them to read our lips."

"Clever girl," Nithercott complimented.

They moved their chairs around and began eating their sandwiches.

Farley grumbled, "This is a waste of time. Alice may be nearby, and we're out here eating cold cuts."

"You need to eat, Farley. You are not yourself. All of us need sustenance to keep going. What good will we do Alice if we are sick?"

Farley took a bite of his sandwich with Nithercott's encouragement.

"That's a good chap. We need food to work to our peak efficiency," Nithercott said.

"Professor, have I ever told you that you are a scruffy mutt?"

"Often. Keep eating, Farley."

"There's something we need to discuss," Mona said.

Both Farley and Nithercott looked expectantly at her.

"Nithercott, this isn't your fight. You should leave."

"And abandon the adventure of a lifetime?"

Farley said, "I agree with Mona. It's an adventure which might get you killed. You were dragged into this by accident. You don't even know Lady Alice."

"I know enough to know I would like to become acquainted with Lady Alice better. Please don't send me away. My entire adult life has been devoted to reading other people's exploits while sitting in a dusty, moldy, sterile, academic building. Now I have the chance to be a hero and save a damsel in distress."

Farley asked, "Is this worth risking your life?"

"Yes, I think it is. Otherwise, what kind of man am I?"

"I hope you won't be a dead one," Farley said.

Nithercott clapped his hands. "Then it's settled."

"Where do we go from here, Mona?"

"I think Alice is in the house. At the very least on the grounds. It would only make sense she is here somewhere."

Farley said, "We searched the house, remember?"

"That thump on the head has scrambled your brains. You and Alice searched the house before she was kidnapped. We haven't searched the house since we came back after the accident. Surely, the message scrawled on my mirror proves the kidnappers are here."

"At least some of them," Nithercott agreed.

"When we came back from the accident, all three of us took to our beds. It's almost two days later and we're still dragging, with Farley having the most difficulty."

"I'm glad someone has noticed."

Mona admonished, "Quit being such a baby. A man at your age."

"Well, there goes the sympathy."

"She's rather hard on us, isn't she?" Nithercott said.

Farley teased, "Mona doesn't like men."

"You think that's it?"

"Quite so. She's resisted me, and I say, what is there to resist?"

"Boys!"

"You have our rapt attention, Mona."

"How many rooms are in Bosworth?"

Farley answered, "One hundred and four, but

most of the rooms are locked. The west wing hasn't been used for years. It seems only the public rooms, some bedrooms in the east wing, and the servants' quarters are in use."

"I'm going to my room," Mona announced.

"No, don't. Obviously your room has been compromised," Farley said, alarmed.

"I'm going up to my room."

"I won't allow it, Mona. It's too dangerous."

"I am perceived as less threatening. If there is going to be actual contact, it will be with me, and I think it will be in my room."

"What if they take you as well?"

"Then you will know Alice and I are both in the house somewhere. The kidnappers are not going to hurt us until they get what they want."

"How do you want to proceed?" Nithercott asked.

"I'll walk into the house first. You both follow a few minutes later. Go to the trophy room and procure the shotguns. Act as though we are preparing for another search."

"Let's do it before it gets dark. I want to be able to see what's coming around the corner at me."

"Farley, if something is coming around a corner, you won't see it anyway."

"Good point, but you know what I mean."

"I'm spooked, too," Nithercott said.

Mona took a deep breath, trying to shake off a feeling of calamity. "I'll be glad when this is over, and I'm home butting heads with my general contractor repairing Moon Manor."

"Shall we go back now?" Farley said. "I want to get this over with. Do you have your pistol, Mona?"

"Yes."

"Nithercott, mind if I talk to Mona alone?"

The Professor noticed Farley's intense expression. "Think I'll go for a quick smoke. Shan't be long."

Farley and Mona watched Nithercott wander off while lighting his pipe.

"What is it?"

"I want to apologize for my behavior after Alice was kidnapped. It threw me, and I lost myself momentarily. I never meant to put you in danger with my drinking."

"I need to count on you, Farley. Alice needs you also. Nithercott means well, but you're the only muscle around. Can I rely on you?"

"Alice and I are over. We've been through for a very long time."

"I wasn't talking about that."

"But I am. I wasn't lying when I told you I hadn't spoken to Alice in six years."

"Your relationship with Alice is none of my business."

"I want to make it your business. I want you to know." Farley grabbed Mona. "Listen, Mona. When this is over, we need to address why you keep pushing me away. I need to tell you how I feel. Let me."

"Are you making a romantic declaration to me?" Mona asked coldly.

"Quit being so unapproachable. I'm trying to explain that Alice and I are not an item."

"Alice says you will come back to England to live once your father passes. She thinks she would be the perfect wife for you as the Duchess of Brynelleth, and I think she's right. I wouldn't do. You know that and I know that, so there's no point in pursuing me any further."

"You can't stand there and tell me you don't care about us. You wouldn't have gotten so angry about the drugs and the drinking if you didn't care."

"I don't really. Now let me go!" Mona pulled away and hurried toward the house. She wouldn't give Farley the satisfaction of seeing her wipe away tears. Mona couldn't wait to depart from dreary England for the rolling green hills of the Bluegrass and leave Lawrence Robert Emerton Dagobert Farley behind.

27

Mona gathered her courage and climbed the darkened staircase, rejoicing when she entered her bedroom without incident. She jumped at every sound not wishing to be hit on the back of the head. If one of the kidnappers was going to make contact, she'd rather have it be a face-to-face, and not wake up helpless in the fiend's lair.

There was some comfort that Farley and Nithercott were collecting shotguns from the trophy room. Still, Mona felt rattled. Farley had picked an odd time to declare his feelings for her. It was distracting, and Mona needed to be on top of her game.

She needed to do something productive, so Mona decided to wipe the message from her dressing table mirror. Mona went into the bathroom and splashed water on her face. Looking in the mirror, she noticed much of the swelling had subsided. At least, that was positive. Grabbing a washcloth, she went back into her bedroom and stopped dead.

A man sat calmly in a chair by the window—a man Mona hated and feared.

"Hello, Marden Sinclair," Mona said, reaching for her gun.

28

"It's been a long time, Mona. Much too long."

"I ought to kill you."

"Ooh, such dramatics, but then Americans are so emotional."

"Keep your hands where I can see them."

"You're not as pretty and fresh as the last time I saw you. You look older and perhaps a little more shopworn. Your expiration date is soon to be up, Mona dear. Better catch a husband before the bloom fades entirely from the rose."

"Keep giving me reasons to kill you."

"If you shoot me, you'll never see Alice again."

"You won't mind if I keep my gun trained on you. My finger on the trigger is reassuring."

"You'd be shooting an unarmed man."

"Where's Alice?"

"Give us what we want, and we'll let her go."

"Who is *us*?"

"Let's just say interested parties."

"Always the messenger boy. Never the boss."

"I'm tiring of this conversation, so I'll take my leave." Sinclair started to rise.

"Don't move."

Sinclair smiled sardonically and slowly stood. "You're not going to harm me. I hold the key to Alice."

"We don't know what we're looking for. Throw us a bone, Sinclair, so we can end this."

"You'll know it when you see it. All I can say is, it is quite small. We know Morrell possessed it before the attack on the compound. He must have gotten it out because we found no sign of it in Iraq. We believe it is here."

Mona moved to intercept Sinclair as he moved toward the hidden door which stood wide open.

"More information," Mona demanded.

Sinclair smiled. "It is interesting you haven't asked how Lady Alice is doing. I could be entertaining all sorts of lovely interaction with her like I wanted to do with you. It was she who interrupted us in Iraq, wasn't it?"

Mona threw off the urge to shudder. "I need proof of life."

Sinclair threw her a piece of fabric. "I think you will recognize this cloth from the dress she was wearing."

Mona let the fabric fall on the floor. "It proves nothing except that you had her. Doesn't prove she is still alive."

"What would you like? An ear? A finger?"

"Please don't do that."

"Ah, now you say please."

"A letter. Bring me a letter. A note written on a newspaper with the date exposed. I know Alice's handwriting. We may find what you want, but we won't turn it over until we see proof of life."

"A tedious request, but I suppose it's acceptable. We will comply." Sinclair scratched the corner of his mouth. "I hear His Lordship and Professor Nithercott coming up the stairs. No doubt they want to inform you the guns from the trophy room have been dismantled."

Sinclair stuck out his lower lip and pouted,

mocking Mona. "So sorry, but it had to be done. A little word of advice. If we see you attempt to leave the grounds, we will cut the phone wires and shoot to kill. Our guns are in working order."

"Wait. Wait! How will I contact you if we find something?"

"Don't worry. We'll be watching. Ta-ta for now, my Mona Lisa."

Sinclair slipped through the hidden corridor door as Farley knocked on Mona's bedroom. Not hearing a response, Farley and Nithercott barged in to see the hidden panel slip into place.

Farley looked questioningly at Mona.

"It was Marden Sinclair."

"And you let him get away!" Farley uttered, rushing to the door.

"Stop," Mona implored, putting herself in front of the door panel. "There are more than one. If he doesn't return, they might hurt Alice in retaliation."

Nithercott grabbed Farley. "Think, man. Think."

Farley shook him off. "Are you all right, Mona?"

"He didn't touch me."

"What did he say about Alice?"

"He's going to bring us proof that she is still alive in the form of a note written on a current newspaper. So, I think we should keep looking for whatever he wants."

Nithercott asked, "Did he say how Alice was?"

"No, but they have her." Mona picked up the piece of fabric. "Here is a section of the dress she was wearing when she was taken."

Farley asked, "Did he say want they wanted?"

Mona shook her head. "He said it was small."

"How many men does he have?"

"I would think no more than three."

Farley asked, "What makes you think so?"

"One to guard Alice and two to keep watch over us. Any more than three would be a tactical mistake. Where would they be getting their supplies? It would have to be cold rations as they couldn't use the kitchen."

"There's also the need for water," Nithercott added.

"They must be stationed in the west wing."

Mona said, "We can't be sure. They certainly know this manor better than we do, and I'm sure they have explored all its hidden recesses. What we need are the original plans of the house."

Farley said, "I doubt they would do us any good. Houses of this size were constantly modified as the years went by. A lord would add and tear down as to his personal preference and the architectural taste of the era."

"You spent a lot of time here, Farley. Can you draw a plan of this house from memory?"

"We played in the corridors as children, but that was twenty-some-odd years ago. I don't remember much about the layout."

Mona decided to change the subject. "What about the guns?"

"Useless. The firing pins have been removed."

Nithercott offered, "I can make a dash for the village."

"No, don't do that. I was told we would be shot if any of us attempted to leave Bosworth Manor."

Farley spat, "That's not jolly."

Nithercott pleaded, "We should call Scotland Yard for help. This is beyond us."

"It's too late. We are in this to the end for better or worse."

Nithercott said, "I think Sinclair is bluffing. Either that or he's got more men than we think he does."

"I think he's deceiving us somewhat, but we can't take the chance," Mona replied.

"Can we do something more than stand around and talk?" Farley barked, impatient for action.

Ignoring Farley's outburst, Mona said, "Sinclair said Colonel Morrell had the object before the attack, and then after they couldn't find it. I think the attack was an attempt to obtain this artifact. In his journal, Morrell wrote that he knows of the impending confrontation and hid the article where they would never find it."

Farley suggested, "Let's start with Alice's room."

"They have already searched her bedroom. Remember the robbery," Mona added.

"The priest hole then," Farley said.

"Alice would have had to discover the object among her father's things and taken it to the priest hole, but she denied knowing what these men wanted. She was just as baffled as we are now."

Nithercott asked, "But what are we looking for?"

Mona answered, "Sinclair said we would know when we found it."

Nithercott mumbled, "That's an idiotic clue."

"It must be spectacular, but small you say?" Farley asked.

"Alice said her father's effects were sent along with his body. She got out a few things, but left the rest in storage."

"Let's start there," Farley suggested.

"Righto," Nithercott agreed. "Where are they?"

"Where does the house store items, Farley?" Mona asked.

"There's a storage room in the basement and some rooms on the third floor. Colonel Morrell also stored items in a barn near the stables."

"We can cover more ground if we split up," Mona proposed.

"No, it's safer if we stay together," Farley insisted.

Nithercott concurred, "I agree."

"Let the games begin," Farley cracked as he followed Mona and Nithercott up to the third floor.

29

They found nothing. It appeared no one had been in the third floor storage room for years. An undisturbed layer of dust confirmed it.

Next they tried the basement where they found boxes of Colonel Morrell's personal effects. They spent hours going through them only to find nothing of great value. They even cut the lining from his clothing looking for hidden pockets. Again, nothing.

Mona sat on a broken hobby horse, wiping a cobweb from her hair. "What do we do now?"

"The barn," Farley suggested.

"Which barn? There are several."

"Are there animals which need our care?" Nithercott asked.

Mona explained, "Alice sold off the horses

and closed down the dog kennels. Any livestock left is taken care of by tenants."

"Would Morrell have sent anything to one of the tenants? Perhaps one he trusted," Nithercott asked.

"Unlikely," Farley said. "Colonel Morrell was not known for his affable rapport with the locals."

Nithercott looked at his watch. "If we're going, we need to make it snappy. Better take torches with us. It's getting late."

Mona remarked, "I thought we'd have found whatever it is by now."

"Don't be discouraged. Plenty left to do," Farley said, pulling Mona off the toy horse.

Mona was tired but put on a brave smile. "Of course." She followed Nithercott up the stairs to the grand hall. Farley brought up the rear, holding a rapier he had found. "Are we going to swash-buckle our way out?"

"Douglas Fairbanks does."

"That's in the moving pictures."

Farley tried to respond, but Nithercott interrupted to ask what their next plan of action would be.

"There are three barns on the property. Let's start with the one closest to the Morrell mausoleum," Farley stated. He glanced at Mona to gauge her thoughts.

She nodded in agreement. "If we don't find anything in the barns, let's knock off for a few hours and get some rest. I'm about done in."

"I could do with a couple of hours of shut eye," Farley said, looking behind him to make sure no one followed.

They hurried to the barn—Farley with the rapier, Mona with her gun, and Nithercott with a flashlight which he found by the front door.

Farley looked up at the moon as it rose above the treeline. "That's not a good omen. The moon is red."

"It's a blood moon, a portent of death," Mona said.

"You two are such jolly fun. Must be a blast at children's birthday parties and weddings," Nithercott remarked.

They arrived safely at the barn. It was old with several cupolas, which housed cooing pigeons angry that humans were invading their domain. Farley and Mona searched diligently while

Nithercott stood guard watching from the hayloft.

Finally, Mona broke down and said, "I've simply got to take a break. Besides, there's nothing here but moldy hay and rusting farm implements."

"Maybe there's a recess in the floors?" Nithercott suggested.

"The floor is dirt. There's nothing here."

Farley took a flask from his pocket and handed it to Mona.

"You promised you wouldn't drink," Mona admonished.

"It's water. I filled it up before we left the house."

"May I have some of that, mate?" Nithercott asked.

Farley handed the flask to Nithercott and watched him take a drink. "What to do now?"

"We must think this through logically," Mona said. "We know it's small. We know Colonel Morrell recognized its importance and hid it before the attack."

"This could be a wild goose chase. Morrell could have buried it in Iraq."

Mona insisted, "I don't think so, Farley. Sinclair and his men exhausted their search in Iraq. If they believe the item is here, they must have solid reasons to think so."

"But where?" Nithercott wondered.

Mona tapped on her thigh, a nervous quirk which helped her to think. "Colonel Morrell is the last person to have this piece in his possession. He wrote down that he knew of the impending attack and hid it where it would not be found. First of all, why did he write the last entry?"

"It must have been for Alice," Farley replied.

"I think so, too. He wanted Alice to read his last entry. You know you are going to be attacked and you might die. Where would you hide a small object you want your daughter to have?"

Nithercott quipped, "I'd swallow it."

Both Mona and Farley stared at Nithercott in surprise.

"What did you say, mate?" Farley asked.

"I would swallow it, if I could, of course."

Mona jumped up and kissed Nithercott on the cheek. "You're brilliant. Simply brilliant."

"Don't I get a kiss?" Farley asked. "He's my

friend. I should get some credit."

Farley and Nithercott punched each other on the shoulder when Mona rummaged through some old tools.

"These should work," Mona announced, holding up a crowbar and a hammer.

"You're not suggesting what I think you're suggesting, are you, Mona?" Nithercott said. He swallowed hard, tugging at his collar.

Farley clapped him on the back. "Looks like we've hit rock bottom, Nithercott."

Mona looked squarely at them and said, "Gentlemen, we are going to rob a grave!"

30

Mona, Farley, and Nithercott stood before the sarcophagus of Colonel Morrell.

Mona turned on the flashlight and held it up so Farley and Nithercott could see in the dark mausoleum.

Farley took a deep breath. "No time like the present," he said, taking the crowbar and inserting it under the heavy lid while Nithercott pushed until he was able to slide it off.

All three peered inside.

The remains of Colonel Morrel, in full regalia, rested in silent repose. Most of the flesh was gone but his hair and fingernails were noticeably longer.

"This is quite good," Nithercott said. "I thought he would be gooey, but he looks quite dry."

"Bodies decompose quickly in the Iraqi heat. That's why Muslims bury their dead within twenty-four hours. Colonel Morrell's insistence that his body be brought back to Bosworth Manor must have caused consternation among the locals."

"We're no better than ghouls now," Farley said, revolted at the thought of disturbing the grave of a fellow soldier and superior officer.

Mona put the flashlight in her mouth and gently pushed Farley aside, so she could lean over and unbutton Colonel Morrell's jacket and waistcoat.

Nithercott pulled up the skeleton's shirt.

Farley extracted the flashlight from Mona's mouth and flashed the light upon the corpse.

Something shimmered brightly as Farley splayed the beam of light across Morrell's remains. He jerked the light back searching for the sparkle. "Look there!"

Just below Morrell's rib cage a gold nugget glowed in the artificial light.

Mona exclaimed, "Nithercott, you were right about the Colonel swallowing something!"

Nithercott leaned over and grabbed the object.

Mona and Farley surrounded him, as Nithercott slowly opened his fist exposing a gold ring.

They stared at the ring in silence until Nithercott said, "Mona, see if there is any writing. I'm trembling too much."

Mona picked up the ring and turned it over exposing a flat surface with writing on it.

"I can't look. Tell me what symbols appear."

Mona used her shirt tail to wipe off detritus and peered closely while Farley shined light on it. "As far as I can make out, it has some sort of star or sun design with letters surrounding it."

"Describe it." Nithercott closed his eyes better to visualize the design.

"There's a circle in the middle with a ring around it."

"Are there triangular cones emanating outward from the disk?"

"Yes. They look like carrots surrounding the circle."

"How many?"

Mona counted carefully. "There are sixteen. What do they mean?"

"The symbol is a star burst called the Argead Star. The sixteen carrot-shaped symbols are sun rays radiating from the circle which is the sun. We think it represents the Sun god Helios who was the patron deity of the Argead dynasty."

"Meaning?" Farley asked.

"Helios was the patron god of the Macedonian royal family for many centuries."

"You mean Alexander's family?" Farley asked, his excitement growing.

"Read me the letters."

Mona wiped the ring again and turned it around so she could view it better. "A. Something that looks like an upside down y. E. Another E. A. V. O. P. O. C. A. There's more, but I can't make it out."

Overwhelmed, Nithercott said, "Let me see it."

Mona handed over the ring. "What does it say?"

"I wish I had my loupe, but I think it reads: ALEXANDER III, KING OF MACEDON."

Mona caught her breath. "I feel I should kneel."

Farley quipped, "Isn't that un-American?"

"This is the royal signet ring of Alexander, a potent symbol of his authority and power. He would have used this as his official seal on laws, edicts, anything to do with matters of state."

Mona elaborated, "The scribes would give Alexander documents sealed with heated wax, and Alexander would press this ring into the wax, basically stating he approved of what was written. No one, but the intended reader, could break the royal wax seal upon pain of death."

"Alexander might use ink or, if he wanted to make a real impression upon the receiver of the dispatch, he would make his mark in blood."

"Blood would certainly get my attention," Farley said.

Mona's fatigue had left, and she could barely contain her excitement. "This ring is of great importance. No wonder Colonel Morrell did everything he could to keep it safe."

Mona's concentration was shattered by a booming voice. "He was a clever badger at that."

Mona, Farley, and Nithercott looked up to see Marden Sinclair standing in the mausoleum's doorway holding a pistol on them. Two disreputable looking chaps holding truncheons stood behind him.

"Where's Alice?" Mona asked.

"Hidden away in that ugly house of hers."

Farley said, "We have the ring. We'll give it to you when we have Alice."

Sinclair scowled. "Let me explain something. I have a gun trained on you three, so you will do as I command."

"The ring will do al-Sharif no good. There is no connection with Iraq to help your master rise to power. The ring only connects Alexander to Macedon, not as lord of Persia. Greece will want it."

"It was plundered from Iraq and it's going back to Iraq. Not to some stuffy museum. It will be used for a greater good," Sinclair said.

"For your murdering, thieving boss al-Sharif?" Farley sneered. "He'll only cause havoc. Or does he plan to usurp the ruling family of Iraq? I don't think the British will let that happen."

Mona stubbornly resisted. "We'll trade the ring for Alice. That was the deal, but we must have proof of life. We still don't know if Alice is even alive. Where's her note?"

"Let me put it this way. You're going to be dead if you don't give me the ring."

Farley pushed Mona behind him. "You're

going to kill us anyway."

"Is that true?" asked Nithercott, looking at Farley. He turned back to Sinclair. "That's not the gentleman's code. A deal's a deal."

"I'm not a gentleman."

"Well, then neither am I," Nithercott said, raising the ring to his lips and swallowing.

"You idiot!" Sinclair screamed and rushed forward.

Farley pushed Mona on the ground and smashed the flashlight against a wall. Only a diminutive light from the blood moon shone through the door.

Mona pulled her gun out, but she couldn't see well enough to pick a target among the group of three men fighting in one corner and the two men battling each other in another. She felt around the floor and made contact with the crowbar. Mona grabbed the bar and sprang forward to help Nithercott, swinging wildly in the dark. She heard a loud crack as the crowbar connected with a shinbone.

A man screamed and fell in pain.

Suddenly, shots rang out and a bright light shone in her face. Mona covered her eyes with her forearm.

"Drop your weapons!"

Mona heard metal hit the stone floor.

"Drop the crowbar, Madam."

"Who are you? I can't see with the light. It's blinding."

The light was lowered, but it still took Mona's eyes several seconds to adjust. She cried out, "Farley! Nithercott!"

"I'm a bit bruised, but all right," Farley answered from the other side of the mausoleum.

"Here, Mona," Nithercott called out.

Mona dropped the crowbar which clattered on the stones. A swarthy little man with a Van Dyke beard moved toward her, holding out a badge. "My name is Hussein al-Jubori. I'm an antiquity agent for the Iraqi government. These fine gentlemen behind me are agents from MI5 and some of my men."

"You're the man from the train!" Mona was stunned. "Now that I see you close up, you seem so familiar to me. I remember now. I saw your picture in the paper once, but you weren't sporting facial hair then. The beard threw me off. You were an associate of Gertrude Bell's and worked with her to establish the museum in Bagdad."

Al-Jubori bowed. "I had the privledge of working with Madam Bell before she passed. We Iraqis owe her much."

"You followed us from the United States. How did you know?"

Al-Jubori gave a ghost of a smile. "It's a long story. Suffice to say I've been keeping tabs on Lady Alice for years in order to locate Alexander the Great's ring. I knew she reached out to you for help, so I made it my business to keep tabs on you."

"The beard makes you a little conspicuous."

The Iraqi agent stroked it, saying, "It is my one vice. I cannot part with it."

Nithercott spoke up. "Lady Alice?"

Al-Jubori shrugged. "We have no idea where they took her."

Nithercott pleaded, "Can your men help us find her? We think she is here somewhere."

"As soon as the ring is secured, we will help search."

Mona bit her lip. "Uh, that's going to be a bit of a wait before we can turn it over to you."

Nithercott stepped forward. "It will be less than twenty-four hours, sir. I'm regular as rain."

The Iraqi agent seemed confused. "What's he talking about?"

Mona whispered into al-Jubori's ear.

He gave a command to his men in Arabic which caused them to disappear into the night.

"What did you tell them?" Mona asked.

"I simply said—castor oil."

Mona burst out laughing as Nithercott swallowed hard.

31

Mona was dressing Farley's wounds when she noticed bite marks. "My goodness. He bit you!"

"Sinclair is not one for the Marquess of Queensberry boxing rules. He's strictly a street fighter."

"This will have to tide you over until we get you to a doctor," Mona said, picking up a bottle of whisky and pouring it over Farley's bite marks.

Jumping up, Farley did a little dance. "My Lord, you're a menace, woman! That hurts!"

"Means the alcohol is working." She bandaged Farley's wounds and helped him slip on a clean shirt.

Violet poked her head in Farley's bedroom. "Miss, the doctor is on his way, and the criminals have been taken to the local jail."

"What about the staff?"

"Everyone is back."

"Where is Nithercott?"

"He is downstairs in the servants' bathroom sucking on a bottle of castor oil. The foreign gentleman is with him."

"Any word on Lady Alice?"

"No, Miss, but the police are still looking."

"Let me know if they find something."

"Yes, Miss." Before going downstairs, Violet noticed Mona lovingly button Farley's shirt. She closed the door behind her, giving the two some privacy.

Mona asked, "Why did you stand in front of me and then push me to the ground?"

"It is simply what a man of quality does for any damsel in danger."

"That's all?"

"That's all. I have a question."

"Shoot," Mona said.

"When the fighting began, you helped Nithercott and left me alone to face Sinclair."

"I knew you didn't need my help whereas Nithercott was in real danger. I mean, Violet could take Nithercott down if she had to."

"That's all?"

"That's all."

Farley breathed a sigh of relief. "When this is over we need to have a serious conversation."

"Oh, don't start that nonsense again."

"How about this?" Farley pulled Mona close and kissed her passionately.

Mona returned Farley's kiss with such ardor, her emotions surprised her. She pressed against him, letting him explore her body and experiencing pleasure she had never known from a previous sexual encounter. Mona wanted Farley, and her desire made her almost swoon at his touch.

Suddenly, a knock on the door sounded and Danny stuck his head in, saying apologetically, "Sorry to interrupt but the men from MI5 are leaving."

"Alice has been found?" Mona said, pulling away from Farley, feeling ashamed at her momentary lack of control.

"No, Miss."

"Leaving?" Farley said, looking astounded at Mona.

He, too, was caught off-guard at the intensity of their encounter.

They both scuttled down the stairs to find al-

Jubori in a heated discussion with the agent in charge and his MI5 colleagues.

"Have you found Lady Alice?" Farley asked.

The MI5 agent said dispassionately, "We found blood in one of the corridors and drag marks to the outside. It is in my opinion the thugs murdered Lady Alice and buried her somewhere on the grounds. We will resume our search in the morning to look for the grave, but there is nothing we can do at the moment."

Mona argued, "But you don't know for sure Lady Alice has been killed. She might be locked away."

"I'm sorry, but we've gone through every room. We will return in the morning." The agent tipped his hat. "Miss. Your Lordship." He motioned to his men to follow.

Mona turned to Farley who said, "Mona, we might need their help tomorrow. Don't anger the blokes. Stand down."

Al-Jubori turned to Mona. "Don't fret, Miss Mona. My men will continue looking for Lady Alice."

"Thank you."

"MI5 has searched the entire house, and they

may be correct in their suspicion Lady Alice has been murdered. The blood in the secret hallway is most disconcerting."

"It may not even be Lady Alice's blood," Mona countered.

Al-Jubori narrowed his eyes at Mona's naïve statement. "Sometimes it is Allah's will."

Mona clasped her hands in despair. "I understand what you're saying, but I'll accept her death when I see a body."

"Your faith is most contagious, so I ask your guidance on where to look."

"Alice told me there was another priest hole in the great hall."

"Then that is where we shall start." Al-Jubori called to his men as Farley rushed to the kitchen to gather the staff to help.

Mona stood in the middle of the great hall, determined to find Alice alive. She turned round and around taking in the surrounding walls, panels, and columns where a clever carpenter, sympathetic to the Catholic cause in the 1500s, could build a room to conceal a priest. Mona would never give up looking for Alice, alive or dead.

32

The manor staff and al-Jubori's agents moved the furniture to the middle of the great hall and took down the tapestries and paintings. Everything lay in a great heap upon the flagstone floor.

Mona, Farley, Violet, George, Danny, the two maids, al-Jubori, and his men spread out at arms length from each other facing the walls.

Mona instructed, "Knock on the wall and listen for a hollow sound and feel with your fingers for a lever or groove of some sort. Reach as high as you can. Search all the way to the floor. Start now. Time may be running out for Lady Alice."

Al-Jubori gave orders to his men in Arabic. They began exploring as did Mona, Farley, Violet, and Alice's staff. After several minutes, they turned, one by one, and faced al-Jubori.

Nothing unusual was found.

Still not giving up hope, Mona had everyone move to the east wall where they searched again, while she and Farley tapped on the great marble columns which bolstered the roof.

"Mona, these babies are solid," Farley said.

Al-Jubori tapped the great flagstones with a cane listening for any unusual sound. He looked at Mona and shook his head.

Tears sprang to Mona's eyes. Could her dear friend really be dead? It was Alice who had saved her from Marden Sinclair. It was Alice who loaned Mona money when she so desperately needed it. It was Alice who invited her to Bosworth Manor for Christmas when Mona had nowhere else to go.

Farley put his arm around Mona. "We are at the end, my dear. Maybe it is time we should accept that Alice is buried somewhere on the grounds."

Mona shook him off. "I can't let Alice go like this. We had a quarrel before she was kidnapped, and we never got the chance to make up. This can't be it for us."

"What was the quarrel about?"

"Something silly," Mona lied, wiping a tear away.

Al-Jubori circled the room to examine the layout of the great hall. "Miss Mona, have you checked the staircase? In Iraq, we use the space under the stairs for storage. I'm sure the English do the same." He stood before the staircase, cocking his head one side to another, pondering where a clever carpenter could hide a secret room within a staircase.

Mona went to him and begged, "Please."

Al-Jubori barked an order, and his men swarmed over the staircase. "I told them to tear it apart if they had to, Miss Mona."

After several minutes of searching, one man cried out to al-Jubori and waved him over.

"He's found a lever," al-Jubori said, glancing at Mona.

Farley took Mona's hand in his. "Whatever we find, we'll face it together."

Mona nodded at al-Jubori to give his man the signal to pull the lever.

The fourth step from the bottom popped up.

Mona squeezed Farley's hand.

An agent peered inside and gestured wildly. Two other men searched the bottom steps and found a latch. The bottom three steps swung open and an entrance to a secret priest hole emerged.

Violet handed Farley a flashlight. He turned, giving Mona an encouraging smile, before he crouched down and entered the opening.

Several Iraqi agents followed inside.

"Mona! Mona! She's here," Farley called out.

George and Danny rushed over with blankets and water.

Farley came out first, followed by the Iraqis who carried Lady Alice and placed her gently in a chair. They cut off coarse ropes that had cut cruelly into her wrists and ankles.

Farley untied the handkerchief around Alice's eyes and pulled a stocking out from her mouth.

"Alice. ALICE! Can you hear me, darling? You're safe. We found you," Mona pleaded. She turned to Farley. "What's wrong? She's not responding."

Al-Jubori pulled Mona away. "Lady Alice has been poorly used. I think they did not give her food nor water since her captivity. She needs fluids."

"We shall take her to a hospital," Farley declared.

Farley helped George wrap a blanket around Alice, while Violet tried to get Alice to sip on water, but Alice choked on it.

"How far away is the hospital?" al-Jubori asked.

"Forty-five minutes, perhaps."

"Lady Alice will fall into a coma before then. Let me and my men help. We know how to resuscitate those who have been lost in the wilderness, and Lady Alice has been in a terrible desert."

Farley picked Alice up. "Where do you want her?"

Mona started to speak.

"Be quiet, Mona. These men are Alice's hope. Al-Jubori is right. They are trained in survival tactics. George, call the village doctor. Tell him to come straight away."

Al-Jubori said, "Bring Lady Alice into the kitchen. We will need a tube."

"I know what you're going to do," Violet chimed in.

"Would a pastry bag do? I saw my mother use

one once to feed a sick puppy. It worked fine."

"That will be good, Miss, uh, Miss?"

"Violet, sir. My name is Violet. Let me assist you, please."

"Very good." Al-Jubori snapped another order at his men. One of them took Lady Alice from Farley and hurried toward the kitchen. "Miss Violet will assist. The rest of you will be in the way."

Mona stepped forward to protest, but al-Jubori wagged a finger at her. "You are too emotional to help. You'll just be in the way." He turned to George. "We need more blankets and towels. Someone needs to show the doctor in when he comes."

Breathless, Danny ran into the great hall. "I contacted the doctor's home. He's delivering a breech baby. Won't be able to come for some time."

"Then it is up to us," al-Jubori said.

George showed al-Jubori and his men the way to the kitchen fluttering around them like a frightened bird.

"Farley?" Mona said.

"The man's right. Stay put. Besides, Nithercott is in the servants' bathroom near the kitchen being fed castor oil. It will be too crowded."

"She looked so pale."

"I trust al-Jubori. If anyone can bring Alice around in this emergency, it's he."

"What shall we do?" Mona asked.

"I'm going to shave and shower. I stink. So should you. You're covered in grime."

"Shower at a time like this?"

"It's better than pacing the floor like an idiot. Alice may have to be transferred to the hospital after al-Jubori stabilizes her. Do you want to speak with her doctor looking like you do? Appearances must be kept up, my dear."

"Stiff upper lip and all that."

"Quite."

Mona threw up her hands and followed Farley up the back stairs to the second floor. She should have been in high spirits. Alice had been found and the culprits were safely in jail, but Mona couldn't quell her anxiety.

Until Alice sat up and spoke, Mona wouldn't rest easily. She whispered a prayer. "Please, God. Help Alice. If for some reason, you take her, tell her I said *Amiens!*"

Amen.

33

Several weeks later as Violet packed Mona's steamer trunks, Alice walked into the room.

"Lady Alice, you shouldn't be up. You're still very weak."

"That beastly sedative Sinclair gave me affected my heart. Now I'm weak as a kitten," Lady Alice said, slipping into a chair, "but I wanted to talk with you, Violet."

"Let me get you a cup of tea, Lady Alice."

"For goodness sake, stay put. This isn't easy for me, but it needs to be said."

"Yes, Lady Alice."

"I want to thank you for repairing my clothes and shoes. I know I was looking rather untidy, and it was kind of you to notice and help in the matter. You're a very clever seamstress."

"It was Miss Mona who suggested I do so."

Lady Alice waved her hand in a dismissive manner. "I know. I know, but you took such care. My clothes will last several more years, if they don't go out of style." She took several items out of her pocket. "I wanted to give these to you."

"No, Lady Alice, Miss Mona has reimbursed me for my time."

"I want to thank you properly myself." Lady Alice tugged on Violet's hand and placed a gold coin in it. "I know your president has ordered a cessation to private ownership of gold, but every woman should have something made of gold tucked away in case of a rainy day. It's worth twenty pounds, so don't lose it. And I want you to have this." Lady Alice handed her a velvet box. "My mother gave me this when I was seventeen. You look about that age now."

"Eighteen."

"I wore these for many years. They are worthy of a woman with pluck. That describes you, Violet."

Violet opened the box. Inside were a necklace, bracelet, and a small pair of matching earrings of brightly painted violets made from ceramics. "This is a perfect ensemble for a young lady about the town."

"I can't accept, Lady Alice. It is too expensive."

"I doubt I will ever have a daughter, Violet. I would like someone to wear this set in honor of my mother and me. Please wear in remembrance of our adventure together."

Violet stared at the jewelry. "I've never had anything so lovely."

Lady Alice closed Violet's hands over the velvet box. "Then it is settled." She glanced at the opened steamer trunks on the floor, and the myriad of outfits laid out on the bed. "Well, goodbye, Violet. If God is willing, we shall meet again."

Violet curtsied. "So long, Lady Alice."

"Oh, my dear, you're so hopelessly American." Lady Alice said, smiling tenderly.

34

Farley and Mona walked among the yew topiaries trimmed in the shape of large triangles in the formal English garden.

"Has al-Jubori sent any word about the rings?" Mona asked.

"No one is talking. Not MI5. Not Scotland Yard. Nada. However, I have some contacts on the local police force. I was told al-Jubori left Great Britain with his men, carrying a diplomatic briefcase chained to his wrist."

"They should return Alice's ring if they found it. It is private property."

Farley said, "She'll have to hire a lawyer, but I doubt she'll ever see that ring again. Al-Jubori will just deny its existence if he has it."

"They should at least reimburse her."

"That would be admitting the Iraqi government has possession of it. I doubt Alice will see a penny."

Mona said, "I wonder if either of those rings really belonged to Alexander. It would be fabulous if one of them did, especially the one I got to hold."

"Poor Nithercott. The Iraqis poured castor oil down his throat until he exploded. I understand it was quite a messy affair."

"How is he?"

Farley answered, "I talked with him this morning. He's back home. Said he lost five pounds the hard way, but the only damage done was to his dignity."

"You said pounds, rather than stones. You're turning into a colonist."

"Perish the thought."

"You said you wanted to speak with me privately," Mona said, watching Farley fidget with his pocket handkerchief. "What is it? We need to hurry. Our ride will be here in less than an hour, and I don't want to be late for the train."

"That's what I wanted to speak to you about. I'm not going back to Kentucky. I can't leave

Alice in such a lurch. After I get her affairs settled, I'm going to visit my father and stay for awhile. He's not well."

Farley's words hit Mona hard, but she maintained her composure. And like any woman of quality, she held out her hand and said, "Alice said your true home was in England. I wish you both well."

"I'm not going to shake your hand like we're strangers, woman. I'll be back in Kentucky before Bob's your uncle."

Mona reached up and kissed Farley on the cheek. "Goodbye, Robert, and bless you."

"Mona, I'm coming back to Kentucky. I swear. Mona. Mona!"

She didn't hear Farley's last words. She choked back tears as she hurried across the garden to Bosworth Manor. She doubted she would ever see Farley again.

Mona's first stirrings of love had been a flop. She did not feel she would ever let her guard down again where romance was concerned.

Romance was for gothic novels written by love-starved maidens who lived on the moors.

Love was not for Madeline Mona Moon.

35

Mona and Violet sat patiently in the waiting room at the station for their train to Plymouth.

Violet hummed Ruby Keeler's hit *Shuffle Off To Buffalo* while reading *Photoplay Magazine*.

Mona sat beside her, nursing a wounded heart. "I won't pine over some man. I won't!"

"What's that, Miss?"

Excitedly, Mona turned to her maid. "Violet, how would you like to see Paris?"

"You mean as in Paris, France?"

"Yes, would you like to see the Eiffel Tower and take a trip to the castle I told you about— Versailles? Eat some French cooking. Drink French wine."

"But the cost, Miss."

"What's the point of money if you don't

spend it on people who matter?"

Violet blushed at Mona's statement. That she and Mona could form a bond besides one of employer and employee was a foreign concept to Violet, but one which pleased her.

After all, Mona was her idol. "I would like to go very much, Miss."

"Then we shall do so." Mona tore up their train tickets and tossed them in the nearest bin. "Let me get new tickets, and it's off to gay Paree. Perhaps we can make an appointment with Gertrude Stein in Paris and see her art collection," Mona mused.

"Who is Gertrude Stein?"

"A rose is a rose is a rose."

"Huh?"

"I'm going to open up a world for you, Violet. Just grab onto my coattails and hang on."

"Yes, Miss." Violet opened her purse and took out Lady Alice's velvet case. Violet quickly put on the jewelry so she would look smart when she arrived in Paris. After checking herself in a compact mirror, she reached for her chest. Her heart was beating like a whirligig in a strong wind. Violet took several deep breaths, trying to soothe her nerves.

Life with Miss Mona will always be a whirl-wind. "I must get used to it and enjoy the spectacle," Violet ruminated.

She saw Mona beckon, holding up two tickets. Violet beamed at her adventurous employer. "I'm ready, Miss Mona," she whispered, squaring back her shoulders.

"What did you say, Violet?"

"I said I'm ready, Miss."

"So am I." Mona removed her silk hat and threw it straight up in the air. "Let the games begin!"

The history is true. WWI was known as the Great War before 1939. Mesopotamia and Near East refer to the Middle East. A priest hole was a secret room where Roman Catholic priests were hidden, usually from 1550 to 1603, after "Catholic" plots were discovered to overthrow the Protestant rule of Elizabeth I. The Act of Supremacy was an oath taken by high-ranking subjects to acknowledge the king or queen of England as supreme ruler and head of the Church of England. The Spanish Flu killed more people in one year than the Bubonic Plague killed in one century. Gertrude Bell was an English cartographer who started the Bagdad Museum and drew the borders for modern Iraq. In Great Britain, articles are sometimes dropped before a noun, such as "I will tell cook." MI6 is British foreign intelligence service and MI5 is a British domestic intelligence agency. The Moon family and Moon Manor are fabrications of my imagination, as are the rest of the characters and Bosworth Manor.

You can check out all the fabulous people and locations mentioned in this story on my Pinterest board for

The Mona Moon Mysteries

pinterest.com/abigailkeam/mona-moon-mysteries

You're not done yet!
Read on for a bonus chapter
from Mona's new adventure!
MURDER UNDER A BAD MOON
Turn the page.

Mona's on the trail of a new adventure.
Time for you to travel back into time!

Keep on going.

1

Mona was in the fields checking on the foals with Kenesaw Mountain, her new farm manager, when Jamison rode up on a truck. "Miss Mona, you gotta come home with me now."

"What's the problem?"

Not wanting to say in front of Mountain, Jamison repeated, "Come on, now. You're needed at home."

Alarmed, Mona asked, "Has anyone been injured?"

"Not that kind of hurt," Jamison replied.

"Sorry, Kenesaw. Gotta go. Finish with the foals," Mona said, jumping into the truck. She didn't have time to complete her instructions as Jamison tore out of the field, leaving ruts in the pristine field.

"Jamison, what is the matter?" Mona asked, holding onto an armrest for dear life.

"Sheriff Monahan is at Moon Manor to arrest you."

Astonished, Mona said, "That's crazy. Whatever for?"

"Sure enough, but he's got his men looking for you. Miss Jetta has called Mr. Deatherage and told me to hide you good until Mr. Deatherage can get here."

"Where are we going?"

"To my sister's house in Bracktown."

Hitting a bump, Mona's head hit the roof of the car. Exasperated, she said "I still don't know what this is about. Why does Sheriff Monahan want to arrest me?"

"He says you done kill Judge Garrett."

Mona gasped, "You mean Judge Garrett is dead?"

"Dead as dead can be. He was kilt, and Sheriff Monahan says you done it because Judge Garrett was thrown into the Kentucky River. Miss Mona, that man was so mean even dead, the dirty waters of the river spat him out."

"Don't tell me. On the banks of Mooncrest Farm."

"Yes'am."

"Perhaps he fell into the river fishing, drowned, and was swept along with the current."

"I don't think so, Miss."

"Why not?"

"Because Judge Garrett was missing his head."

"Oh, dear. Sounds ghastly."

"And that ain't all. His head was found in a bucket near one of our back feed sheds. You is in trouble, Miss Mona, and so is everyone who works for ya. They'll pin the blame on one of us working folk as your compatriot. Just wait and see. Sheriff Monahan is dirty as dirt."

Mona leaned back in her seat. She wasn't surprised Garrett was dead or that someone had murdered him. Judge Garrett was a nasty piece of work. His wife left him, his children disowned him, his neighbors despised him, and even his dog loathed him.

It was the dog which started the battle with Judge Garrett.

That damn dog.

MURDER UNDER A BAD MOON

The Josiah Reynolds Mysteries

Josiah Reynolds is a beekeeper who loves her bees, her art collection, and a one-eyed Mastiff named Baby. She lives at the edge of a cliff on the Kentucky Palisades in a mid-century marvel called the Butterfly. She has everything–money, a great husband, lots of friends–until one day she loses it all. Now Josiah's broke, divorced, and discovers she has a knack for finding dead bodies in the land of Thoroughbreds, bourbon, and antebellum mansions where secrets die hard and the past is never past.

The Last Chance For Love Series

After her divorce, Eva Hanover leaves New York City and heads for the Florida Keys. She buys a rundown motel in the seediest part of Key Largo, intending to restore it to its mid-century glory. As Eva refurbishes the motel, the magic of love returns and guests find a second chance at life.

The Princess Maura Tales

Princess Maura must fight and destroy Dorak, the Aga of Bhuttania, in order to free her people from tyranny. She must put aside her own feelings to win a war and restore order, even if it means killing the great love of her life. Danger, romance, and adventure follow Maura as she navigates the treacherous world of Kaseri where evil wizards morph into dragons, a mysterious race of bird-people train her to be a warrior, and an ancient plant gives her magical powers to overcome her enemies.

About The Author

Please don't forget to leave a review at place of purchase and tell your friends about Mona.

Join my mailing list at: www.abigailkeam.com

Join my VIP FB – Abigail's Queen Bees

You can also reach me at Instagram, Twitter, Goodreads, YouTube, and Pinterest.

Thank you again, gentle reader, for your review, which is so important for any book. I hope to meet you again between the pages.